LISTEN

For Derek

LISTEN

NANCY COFFELT

WestSide Books
Lodi, New Jersey

Published by WestSide Books
60 Industrial Road
Lodi, NJ 07644
973-458-0485
Fax: 973-458-5289

Library of Congress Control Number: 2009930787

International Standard Book Number: 978-1-934813-07-2
School ISBN: 978-1-934813-23-2
Cover illustration by Michael Morgenstern
Cover design by David Lemanowicz and Chinedum Chukwu
Interior design by David Lemanowicz

Printed in the United States of America
10 9 8 7 6 5 4 3 2 1

First Edition

LISTEN

PART 1

Will's Blog: I decided I was going to do this online journal thing a while ago, but I wanted to read what other people wrote. I saw some things that got me—they were actually kind of interesting—and some weird stuff, too. Some of it freaking weird. But really, a lot was just boring. That made me feel better about doing this. No one can go through and read all of it, and even if they did, there's so much that I have to say, they'd be too numb or asleep to care what I had to say.

So what am I going to say? Not my name. No way. Not where I live, not where I go to school. But I will say something about who I am. Here's one thing I think that anyone who really knew me would know: I talk to myself. A lot. I always have. It doesn't seem that weird to me. I mean, if I didn't do it sometimes, who else is going to listen to me? My brother used to. But after he became what he became, that didn't happen too much. When he still was around, he'd sneak up on me when I was talking to myself and scare the whatever out of me. He'd call me two steps from crazy. You know what? Crazy is fine with me. But not stupid. Like I said, I'm not giving out any personal information, not so there'd be any way to know who I am. There is no way I'd let anyone I know read any of this, ever.

Another thing—I'm not going to use swear words in my writing. That's because I have this reaction that keeps me from using them. For me, a lot of words have tastes. Like *word*, for example. It tastes like cornflakes. The flavor's more like cornflakes in milk, though, not cornflakes by themselves. They taste completely different.

I've looked it up and found out that other people have this reaction, too. It's called synesthesia. But unlike me, most of them see different colors when they look at letters or numbers. Not as many have this taste deal like I do. But at least there are some others, and in a way, it makes me feel more connected to other people. And that makes me feel better about it.

Sometimes things taste like what they look like. *Blue* tastes inky. That's the best way I can describe it. And *pond* tastes like bad water. So I don't always get good tastes with words. Like with the swear words. None of those taste good. Some taste like what you'd scrape off the bottom of your shoe. Or vinegar, or burnt meat, or—anyway, let's just say they're all nasty.

My brother used to ask me about it. He'd write down what I'd say about a word's flavor. And then he'd ask me again, way later, to see if I gave him the same answer. He was always surprised when I did. He didn't get that the taste *was* the word, not a description of it. I guess maybe it's something you only understand if it's a part of you, if you're born that way like I was. Like when someone tells you about something funny that happened and when you don't laugh, they say you had to be there. This word-taste stuff's kind of a "you had to be there" sort of thing.

That's all I'm going to write now, I guess. I have to go to the store. I'm out of milk, and the only banana that's left on the counter, well, I'm pretty sure bananas are supposed to be yellow, not black. I've been doing the shopping for what feels like forever now, so you'd think I'd be better at keeping food and soap and toilet paper around, but I'm not. It's just too hard to care about all that stuff. And I hate going to the store, especially the closest one. It makes me think about too many things I don't want to remember.

At least the car's running again. Maybe I should get a better one, like one that isn't a trashed station wagon with a crunched-in door. And maybe one that's a better color than dirt or mud-brown. But that seems like too much trouble, and anyway, it runs.

So that's it. I'll end my first post with one of my favorite words. People think it's a sad one, but not me. It tastes like lemon honey.

The word is *good-bye*.

As the car rolled slowly down the street, Carrie's hands clutched the old sedan's oversized steering wheel in the classic ten o'clock and two o'clock positions. Her eyes swept over the green lawns to her left. A boy on a bike whizzed by, startling her and a young man on foot as he came dangerously close to them. A mud-colored station wagon, door dented in and missing its side mirror, came in from the right at the intersection and stopped short with a screech of brakes to let her and the bike pass. Too much activity here, she decided and drove on, past the boy on the sidewalk, to try the next street over.

She scanned and rejected the vista of plastic pools, swing sets, and assortments of playthings before settling on what she'd been trying to find.

"Pull over," said Mavis. She, too, had spotted the small moving figure.

"Quiet," warned Carrie, and she maneuvered to the curb, shifted into Park, popped the door handle, and stepped out of the idling automobile.

"Here," she called in a high, quiet voice. She extended her hand in a beckoning gesture. "Come here." She gave the fronts of her thighs a couple of pats.

"Hurry!" Carrie could hear the urgency in Mavis's voice, even through the windows of the car. Carrie looked right and left down the deserted street and lunged. Then, holding the struggling bundle close with her left arm, she pulled the car door open with her right hand and closed it carefully after her.

"Let's get out of here," growled Mavis. Carrie twisted her body in order to set a bewildered little dog on the seat next to her and turned to address Mavis in the back.

"I told you to be quiet," said Carrie sternly. "Now sit!"

Mavis laid her ears back in apology and slammed her hindquarters down on the seat. Carrie put the car back in Drive, then pulled carefully into the street.

"Who are you?" To Carrie, the dachshund didn't seem to be aware that the words were coming from her own mouth.

"Friends," Mavis offered from the back seat.

"Mavis," Carrie met the German shepherd's eyes in the rearview mirror before returning her attention to the little dog in the front seat.

"We're friends," she said, giving the dachshund a pat before driving back out of the neighborhood.

The boy walked home from school alone. He was heading toward a house, actually. In no way did it feel like home. His backpack swung from his right hand, skimming the pavement in bumps along the sidewalk in time with his dragging steps.

"Kurt rhymes with dirt!" yelled a voice, and a bike sped by, close enough to lift the boy's straw-colored hair in the breeze it created as it passed.

Kurt didn't bother to look to see who it was; it didn't matter, anyway. Beat up that one, and there'd be six more waiting next time. It would have been a satisfying thing to pound him into a nose-weeping pile of pain. But after what had happened before, well, it was probably best just to let it go.

Continuing down the cracked sidewalk past the houses in their jumble of styles and colors, he paused at the corner as he noticed a new flyer stapled to the telephone pole. *That's new.* His mom used to call him "The Noticer" because he noticed everything, even when he didn't want to.

"Lost Cat," the flyer read, above a fuzzy color copy of a calico, then "Reward" and a phone number. Kurt's interest surged at the thought of a reward. He looked up and down the street to make sure no one was looking, then ripped the flyer from the pole. He folded it hurriedly and shoved it in the pocket of his jeans.

Kurt reached his grandmother's house two blocks later and stood on the floor of the sun-heated porch, eyes scanning the area for a truck with oversized tires or its driver, even though he knew full well that he was the only one there.

Dead. He reminded himself. *He's never coming back.* But making sure always helped him to relax, so he let himself take one more look up and down the street.

He could hear the television before he swung open the door, and it took him only a second or two to recognize the bleeps and catcalls as coming from the talk show his grandmother watched. He had no idea, from the raucous laughter and the almost continuous bleeps, what the topic was.

"Hi, Grandma." The woman seated in the chair looked up and smiled in the dimness of the living room. He frowned a little in return. "It's so dark in here," he said. The cave-like closeness made him feel a little on edge, and that edginess made him remember how much he hated the kid who'd hassled him on his way back from school. Kurt walked over to pull open the drapes, making the dust motes rise and whirl in the sudden rays of sunlight. For a moment, Kurt forgot the boy on the bike, the flyer, and everything else. For that one moment, there was nothing but peace and the dance of those brilliant, tiny stars.

∼

Will's Blog: Writing things down is different from talking to yourself. It makes you think more about what you're going to say. When I'm talking to myself, I'm never worried how it's going to sound; it's just me listening, right? So it takes a lot longer to get things out in writing or in speaking to someone else. Like there's this girl, Claire. She has this great red-brown long hair, and she runs by where I live. She also wears these little shorts. I can't stop thinking about those shorts.

She's in one of my classes. We've talked before, but not really about anything. Just stuff the class is about. All I'm able to come up with when she is standing in front of me is something like "Yeah, that's going to be a hard paper to write." How she could resist such wit is amazing. Why can't I say something at least a little cool, or funny enough to make her laugh? Because I'm a loser, that's why.

Like two days ago. "Will," she says, and I'm so happy that she actually said my name, and I'm trying hard to focus on her words, but she looks so good. And when she starts talking about the assignment and deadlines, all I'm thinking about is asking her if she wants to go running together. But do I ask her? No.

"Yeah," I said to her, which wasn't easy because my mouth was so dry, my tongue was sandpaper. "That's going to be a tough assignment." Too bad my tongue wasn't too dry to taste the word *assignment*. It's pretty foul. And it's too bad you can't kick yourself in the ass when you say something so stupid. Funny, but the words *assignment* and *ass* have the same disgusting taste, and I get to relive them both here all over again. Lucky me. See? That's a good enough reason for me not to swear.

I'm so lame. But I can't stop thinking about Claire and those shorts. I dropped all my sports this year, but I know I can still run, I think. I can't be out of shape that soon, right? I mean, I'm not all flabby or anything, so that's got to count for something.

I would like to ask her to hang out, too, but I know she's still 17. I'd be 17 in my senior year, too, if it wasn't for Mrs. Beggs. She's the one who changed all that when she held me back a year. She didn't listen when I told her I wanted to read and that I could spell. She just didn't understand that it took me longer because I was thinking about the tastes. Nobody, not my mom even, ever seemed to want to hear about that. So I got left back.

That means I'm an 18-year-old senior. And I'm pretty paranoid about the whole dating a minor thing, even though I know it's not a big deal. But yeah, I'm paranoid. *Paranoid*. That's a funny one. It tastes like pears, and I like pears, so the taste of that word has always made me feel ambivalent about it—I like pears, but who likes being paranoid? Anyway, running isn't a date. And maybe I *am* too paranoid, but after the deal with my brother, I don't want to give anyone a reason to think I'm the same as him, not in any way.

I'm going now. I'm supposed to be reading and correcting this kid's paper. I signed up for student mentoring because my advisor said it would look good for college.

What a joke all that is. Like putting yourself out to make sure some failure doesn't eff up anymore makes you a better candidate? Right. With this kid, Kurt, I'm doing more correcting than reading. I don't think he's from around here, and I have no idea where he came from. But I do know one thing. Wherever it was, they don't teach spelling there.

Maybe I'll do it. I'll ask Claire tomorrow. About running, I mean. I wish the word Claire had a taste, but it doesn't. *Tomorrow*, though, tastes like tomatoes. I don't know why. It just does.

Carrie pulled the car up the long driveway toward the darkened house. Her twin headlight beams played across the flat screen of the garage door before it lifted with a hum and let them enter. Mavis awoke with a start at the sound of the garage door opening and sat up to shake her head and ears. The dachshund, alert now, too, stood up on short legs to peer out the car windows. Carrie reached over to grab an animal carrier off the passenger floorboards.

A marmalade tabby spoke to her through the wire gate of the carrier. "Where are we?" he queried, with a fang-baring yawn and a stretch. He blinked, and Carrie could see that he had some sort of irritation in one eye. It was nothing a little antibiotic ointment couldn't take care of, and she made a mental note to pick some up at the drugstore the next day. The small black-and-white cat said nothing from its own plastic-and-wire cage and simply stared at Carrie with big round eyes of its own.

"Where are we?" repeated the dachshund.

"Hold on, let me get the light," said Carrie. She lifted both carriers from the car and walked a few steps to the switch on the wall. The dachshund jumped down after her. A light flared from the ceiling, and the garage door began its descent. She returned to the car and opened the back door for Mavis. A curl of the German shepherd's lip let the dachshund know who went first.

"We're home," said Carrie.

"Home?" the dachshund looked up at Carrie from the concrete floor of the garage.

"When's dinner?" asked the black-and-white cat.

"When's dinner?" echoed the dachshund.

Carrie opened the gate of the carrier. The tabby stalked out, scarred ears twitching, ignoring the two dogs. Carrie gently picked up the black-and-white cat, taking it out of the carrier. It felt soft and warm in her arms. "I'll get you some food. Let's go." She closed the car door with a shove of her hip. At the mention of food, the dachshund ceased her questions and followed Carrie, Mavis, and the cats into the house. Another flick of a light switch illuminated the kitchen and a three-legged gray cat whose green eyes were set in a glare.

"Carrie," he said.

Carrie walked past the cat.

"You promised. You said no more rescues after Belle."

Carrie went to a cupboard and opened it to pull down two cans.

"Stop, Carl," she said. The gray cat's ears lay down for a second before springing back up into their twin triangles.

16

The electric can opener whirred, and Carrie set food out in the row of dishes at her feet. Her tone changed.

"Here, Carl, have some din-din," she cajoled. The two dogs, the tabby, and the little black-and-white cat eagerly attacked the fragrant lumps of canned food.

"Din-din," sniffed Carl. But he sauntered over anyway, his belly swinging to the rhythm of his three-beat gait.

"Waste not, want not," said Carrie.

Carl replied to her remark with a flick of his tail, then joined the others, digging into his own food dish.

Kurt's grandmother was asleep in front of the television. She had gotten up from her recliner to share a supper of fish sticks and crinkle-cut fries with him but had returned to her chair as soon as the dishes were cleared. It was her show night, he knew, but he'd never seen her stay awake long enough to watch them all.

At dinner, Kurt had picked at the limp potatoes. The ones printed on the plastic bag always looked so crisp, the shining golden brown of their baked skin promising something entirely different from the reality—wet glue that even the dishwasher on the heavy-duty cycle had trouble scrubbing off. He scraped most of them into the brown paper garbage bag under the sink, feeling more than a little cheated by the frozen food company. He shrugged. He'd had that feeling plenty of times before.

"Put some chicken nuggets and French fries in the oven for yourself," his mom had said more times than he wanted to remember. "You go ahead and eat, and we'll watch a show together later." But usually he had ended up just going to his room after dinner. It seemed like the better choice, especially with some of the people going in and out of the house so many nights back then.

Kurt walked into the living room and listened to his grandmother's steady breathing. Sound asleep, and it was barely eight o'clock.

He reached over to the hooks by the front door to check his grandmother's sweater pockets for spare change. If he had a little bit of cash, then he could get some real fries at the fast-food place in town. Armed now with a newly found wrinkled dollar bill and a handful of change, he reached for the doorknob, then turned at the last moment to slip a couple of cigarettes from his grandmother's pack on the end table next to the recliner. Kurt put a smoke behind each ear, then silently stepped out into the freedom of the still-warm spring evening.

Could be a lot worse, Kurt thought as he headed toward the main street. He took one of the cigarettes from behind his right ear and felt in his jeans pockets for a light.

Crap, he thought, *it's gotta be at home*. He replaced the cigarette. *I guess it is worse after all*. He crossed the convenience store parking lot, stepping over a crumpled paper cup lying on the cracked asphalt, then walked past the electric eye at the door and into the fluorescent world.

He passed the rack of gum and breath mints on his way to the disposable lighters and stopped, feeling the weight of the change in his pocket and weighing the options of his limited purchasing power. Gum could come in handy, he thought, aware of the tobacco smell making its way from behind his ears and beneath his shaggy hair. He chose a pack of Wintermint, mostly because the shimmering stars on the label reminded him of the display of light he'd witnessed earlier in the day. When his dad used to take him fishing, the water had sometimes looked like that, like there was a universe of fireflies flitting just below the surface. When he was little and insisted on touching it, his dad had cuffed the back of his head.

"You'll scare the fish, boy," he'd said. Kurt had retrieved his baseball cap from the bottom of the metal boat and didn't try it again. The time alone with his dad was something he hadn't been willing to risk over some stupid sparkles that only he could see. He'd learned to ignore the teasing flashes and winks after that.

He'd also learned to ignore the pinpoints of light that danced in front of his eyes against a bright sky. Seeing sparkles in the air was something he thought everyone could do. Odd looks and the threat of punishment for lying quickly told him that wasn't the case.

Later, in middle school, Kurt had searched the Web and discovered exactly what those little lights squiggling across his visual field were: *blue field entopic phenomenon*. Kurt found the name as beautifully mysterious as the sparkles themselves. And technically he'd been right to think that everyone could see them because everyone has them. But you had to notice them to see them.

Was he really the only person in the world that noticed, he'd wondered? That thought had made him feel even more alone than he already did.

Kurt noticed the clerk at the register watching him, so

he smiled politely and held up the gum. The clerk gave a wary smile back. As soon as the clerk looked away again, Kurt snagged a plastic lighter hanging in the next display and shoved it into his pocket.

Loser, he thought.

"Thank you," he said to the clerk as he paid for the gum. Kurt walked out past the electric eye again, the French fries no longer a priority. Now all he cared about was finding a sweet place to enjoy a couple of smokes. With the glare of the store's lights and the tuneless Muzak behind him, he made his way into the night once more.

Will's Blog: I tried a run tonight. It wasn't that bad. I only started sucking air at the end. But that was four miles into it. So, not too bad. I'll ask her. To run, that is. I will.

I saw that Kurt kid tonight, too. I guess the work I gave him wasn't enough to keep him busy. Guess I'll just have to give him more next time. I stopped at the store for a bottle of water—there was no way I was making it home without a drink. He didn't even notice I was there. He was too busy making sure the guy at the counter didn't see him throw that lighter into his pocket. What a little creep. I should have given a heads up to the clerk and let him straighten the kid out. I wouldn't have minded seeing that at all.

Maybe if somebody'd done that with my brother when he was Kurt's age, he'd have turned out different. Well, it wasn't my job. Obviously, our dad didn't think it was his, either. It's a little hard to do that from four states away anyway, and it's even harder after you're dead. So was it my mom's responsibility to straighten him out? I don't know. The words *job* and *my mom* never really went together. And those words couldn't taste any more different from each other, either.

Oh yeah, and here's the weird thing. That kid lit a cigarette and then ripped a flyer off the pole out in front of the store. Why would someone do that? I mean, you look at a flyer and then you keep going. You don't take it down. He really is a little creep. He took off, and I finished my water.

Cigarette = taffy. I know. That one always made me wonder, too.

The footstool felt soft under Carrie's tired feet. She stretched out in the big overstuffed chair and closed her eyes. The orange tabby and the black-and-white cat, full now, were curled up together on her knees, and Carl used his funny tripod hop to sit on her ankles. The two sleeping cats started, but then relaxed again into their naps.

"Move over, Carl." Carrie wiggled her toes. Carl muttered something under his breath, but moved his bulk to one side of the footstool. Mavis, followed by the dachshund, entered the living room. Even with her eyes shut, Carrie could hear their toenails clicking across the hardwood floor.

"This is my rug," Mavis said, turning around three times to land with a thud on the large square of shag carpeting.

"Okay," said the dachshund.

"Don't worry," said Carrie. "I'll get you one, too."

They all sat in silence before the dachshund spoke again.

"How am I talking?" she asked.

"It's her," said Carl.

"I'm awake, Carl, I can hear you," said Carrie, even though her eyes were still closed.

"I just listen to you, is all," said Carrie. "It's as simple as that."

"Oh." The dachshund didn't sound convinced. "Is that why I'm here?"

"We saved you, stupid," growled Mavis.

"Mavis," Carrie warned. She opened her eyes and stifled a yawn. "You had a bad home," explained Carrie softly.

"I did?" The dachshund's eyebrows knit together in a frown of concentration.

"I saw you. You and these two, here." Carrie reached down to pet the sleeping cats. "I saw how those people treated you."

"They fed me," offered the dachshund. "I had my own food dish."

"Did they pull your ears?" asked Carrie. "They let you wander around loose. Anything could have happened to you."

"Just the small ones pulled my ears."

"No one should pull your ears," corrected Carrie. "You're safe now."

"Okay," the dachshund replied.

"What do I call you?" asked Carl. His soft rasp of a voice was almost drowned out by the snores of the now sleeping Mavis.

The little dog cocked her head. "Call me?"

"You need a new name—new life and all," said Carl.

"I do?" She looked worried now.

"Your tag said Cocoa, but you don't look like a Cocoa to me," Carrie said thoughtfully. "Maybe they named you that because they thought you were brown, but you're not really. You're more of a copper color, like a penny."

"That sounds good," said the dachshund.

"What does?" asked Carrie.

"Penny," answered the dachshund.

"Penny, I like that," Carl announced. "It's certainly better than Maaaaavis."

"Don't make me come over there, Carl." But Mavis didn't bother moving off her rug.

Carrie reached out and stroked the rough coat of Penny's long back.

Kurt took the stolen lighter out of his pocket and lit the first cigarette before he reached the edge of the parking lot, stopping for just a second to rip down another flyer for the lost cat off a telephone pole. He drew the smoke into his lungs, then began walking eastward. The last tiny glow of light was gone from the sky, but Kurt didn't mind walking in the dark. He liked the feeling of privacy it gave him. He kept a brisk but easy pace, too new a smoker to feel out of breath yet. He thought of his wheezing grandmother, but quickly dismissed it. She was *old*.

His mom had smoked—plenty. Not his dad, though.

When his parents were still together, he'd heard them fighting about it. They'd fought about a lot of things. He'd hated it then, but thinking about it now, it really wasn't more than raised voices. Compared to the smashed lamps and the holes put through doors and walls after Mark moved in, it just didn't seem like that big of a deal. He wondered why, if it wasn't such a big deal, did his parents break up? They sure had never explained that one to him. And asking them about it never seemed like an option.

He took another drag of the cigarette, and the smoke from his exhale followed him like a pale shadow as he continued walking east. He wondered how long it would take to walk across the state—or even two or three. He slowed his onward trudge for a moment. Maybe he really didn't need money for a bus ticket. Maybe he could just walk to his dad's. Yeah, right. Maybe, if he had all summer, he could. He stopped completely and patted his back pocket before pulling out the crumpled flyer. Without the aid of streetlamps, he could barely make out the faded print that read "Lost Cat." He thrust it back in his pocket and thought about taking down the rest of the flyers before anyone else had a chance to find the cat. "Reward," it said. *A reward is a good thing*, thought Kurt. Like his new lighter. That was a kind of reward.

Flicking the butt of the second cigarette from his fingers, Kurt thought about heading back to his grandmother's house. He wasn't wearing his watch, but he knew it must be closing in on ten o'clock. The sidewalk had run out long ago, and the quiet two-lane highway had few houses along it. Small pastures were dotted with the dark shapes of cows and horses, and every once in a while, Kurt heard a dog barking from a driveway as he passed. He looked up at a glow through the trees. The moon was rising, and Kurt could now see shadows all around. He turned and faced his own shadow stretching down the road before him. It was getting late. A rustle in the brush beside him made him jump. But then Kurt saw a pair of glowing eyes peering from the tangled branches. He took a breath, attempting to slow down the runaway train in his chest. *It's just a cat.*

"Here, kitty," called Kurt. He was glad now to have a little company. The cat emerged into the moonlight, its calico spots dark against the light reflecting against its coat. *It's the cat!* Kurt could feel the folded square of paper in his back pocket. "Reward," it said.

"Here, kitty; here, kitty, kitty." Kurt began advancing toward the cat. He tried to keep his voice quiet, but his excitement was clearly spooking the calico. The cat returned to the bushes, and Kurt stood up on his toes to see it come out on the other side, making its way toward the lights of a distant house. He plunged into the brush after it, moving the small branches away from his face and pulling vines and brambles from his jeans. Breathing hard now, he cleared the undergrowth and sprinted up the rise after the cat.

"Here, kitty; here, kitty," panted Kurt, keeping his voice as low as he could manage. The cat suddenly stopped at a small stand of trees near the farmhouse.

"Good kitty," he breathed. He reached out his hands, and the cat made a flirty zigzag toward him.

"Gotcha!" said Kurt as his arms closed around the cat.

The startled animal seemed to decide all at once that this was not at all the place it wanted to be. Its strong back legs kicked furiously against his chest, and Kurt winced at the sting of the sharp claws—*That's going to leave a mark*—but the thought of the reward allowed him to disregard the pain.

Kurt gripped the cat tighter and turned back in the direction of the road. But before he could take even one step, a heavy shape hurled itself from the darkness and slammed him flat to the hard ground at the base of a tree. The calico, free from its captor, rapidly scaled the trunk behind Kurt's dazed head.

He lay wide-eyed, staring at the dog, whose front feet were planted squarely on the scratches across his chest. The huge head of the German shepherd, with all of its teeth bearing menace, was only inches from his face. Kurt stopped breathing and fought mightily against an urge to pee his pants.

"Mavis!" came a woman's voice from the yard. Kurt could hear hurried footsteps approaching over the deep growls of the dog. "Mavis, off!"

The dog stepped off his chest and to the side, and the woman bent down to help Kurt to his feet. "Are you all right?"

Kurt nodded, stunned, as he took in the trim middle-aged woman before him, her white hair a glowing halo in the moonlight. The glow began to blur, and he was suddenly and painfully aware that the breath had been knocked out of him. His ears began a high, ringing buzz, and instead of seeing his usual sparkling pinpoints of light, he saw great circles of black that brought him to nothingness.

~

Will's Blog: Maybe I should get a cat or something, so then I wouldn't have to type or yammer to myself to feel like I'm talking to someone, like I'm not here all alone, even though I really am. But then what would I do with a cat when I leave in the fall? I think my mom would have liked having one. A cat, I mean. Someone to hang out with her all day. The cat probably would have liked it, too, with her being in bed most of the time. I've never had a cat, but don't they sleep all day? I guess I could still talk to a sleeping cat. But they kill things when they're finally awake, don't they? No, now that I'm thinking about it, maybe I don't really want a cat after all.

You know what? Seeing that Kurt kid really bugged me for some reason. It's gotta be more than just him being a jerk, taking the lighter, and ripping down a stupid flyer. I mean, so what? Why does that bother me so much?

He does make me think of my brother, though. Now, don't get me wrong. Even though I'm only two steps from crazy myself, I know this kid's not my brother. He doesn't look anything like him, first of all. My brother didn't have light hair in high school like that kid does, and he didn't have plain, dirt-brown hair like me. You know, I just realized that my beater station wagon and my hair are the same ugly color. I wonder if anyone else seeing me getting out of it has thought the same thing. I wonder if Claire has. I really should get a different car.

Anyway, my brother had this curly black hair in high school, and he always had all these girlfriends. Sometimes it seemed like he had three or four of them at the same time. And there were always a bunch of them hanging at our house. Some of them were even nice to me and didn't give me that "get lost" look or, worse, make some comment so everyone would laugh. And then I'd have to go away so no one could see that I really was a crying little nothing.

My brother could have stopped all that teasing if he'd wanted to. He knew it, but he didn't. He'd rather laugh at me, too, like that made him some kind of big man in front of the girls or something. I don't know why I keep thinking about that, either. It doesn't do any good. It doesn't change anything. I never would have done that to him—been cruel, I mean. Not that he would have cared much if I'd tried. My mom? She was never like that to me that I can remember. But letting my brother and his friends treat me like that and not doing anything about it? Isn't that a kind of cruelty?

The word that keeps coming into my head is *betrayal*. That word tastes like coffee, but not like a coffee drink, like a mocha or something like that. No, *betrayal* is the bitter black sludge waiting in the bottom of your cup, waiting for you to gulp it and spit it right back out.

Carrie sat on a kitchen chair, facing the boy. Thank god, he'd started gasping for breath right away. He was shorter than she was, couldn't be more than five-four, maybe five-four and a half. And although it looked like he wouldn't tip the scales at any more than, say, 110 pounds, she still would've had a hard time getting him in the house by herself if he hadn't been able to walk on his own after Mavis flattened him.

The boy sat across the table, arms crossed, blue eyes steady, ignoring the steaming cup of tea Carrie had nuked in the microwave. "I want to leave," he said.

"Not until you tell me what you were doing on my property," replied Carrie.

"He was stealing Belle!" stated Mavis. "She told me so."

"Why in the world would you steal Belle?" said Carrie, dismissing the dog's remarks with a wave of her hand. The boy eyed Mavis warily, then addressed Carrie.

"I wasn't stealing anything."

"He *had* Belle," insisted Mavis.

"Is it true, then?" Carrie pressed. "You had Belle and were taking her?"

"Let him go, Carrie," advised Carl. He limped over and sprang up into her lap, using it as a platform to reach the surface of the kitchen table. Carl planted himself between Carrie and the kid. The boy stared at the three-legged cat.

"I thought it was a different cat," said the boy. He rose suddenly in his chair. Carl startled at the movement and gave a quick hiss. Mavis and Penny, with ridges of hair raised on their backs, rumbled growls.

"Mavis, Penny, it's all right," said Carrie.

The boy carefully pulled a wrinkled piece of paper from his back pocket and smoothed it out on the table. Mavis and Penny crowded in closer to look, and Carl planted his fuzzy backside practically on top of the sheet. Carrie saw the blurry picture of Belle, even through the creases.

"Is Belle your cat?" asked Penny.

Mavis gave a low growl.

"Well?" asked Carrie, as the boy shifted slightly away from the two dogs and Carl. "Do you think Belle is your cat?"

"No, she's not my cat," said the boy.

"Then why take her?" asked Carrie.

"He's a thief," growled Mavis. "And he smokes, too."

"You're a thief?"

The boy shook his head.

Carrie leaned over the table and gave a sniff. "But you *are* a smoker." She eyed him for a moment. "You look kind of young to be a smoker."

The boy jabbed his finger at the piece of paper in front of him. "I was taking her to get the reward!"

Carrie broke out into peals of laughter. Startled again, Carl leapt off the table and stalked out of the room.

"Money?" she asked as she caught her breath. "You did it for the money?"

The boy nodded.

"What's your name?" asked Carrie.

"Kurt," the boy answered, after a few seconds.

"Kurt," she said, "we need to talk."

Kurt watched the big sedan drive away down the deserted street after Carrie had dropped him off in town. Passing by the bank, he glanced up at the digital sign. It read 54 degrees, and he was surprised to see that the time was 11:43. He walked faster. It really *was* late. He walked along, thinking about the deal she'd offered him.

The money sounds pretty good, he thought. Kurt reached into his front pocket and felt the two folded twenties. Carrie had paid him *not* to return the calico. It *did* sound like she was giving it a better home. She had told sad stories about Mavis coming from the animal shelter and Penny being neglected. And poor three-legged Carl—*Man, what happened to him?*

Forty bucks an animal. Kurt thought Carrie's whole "save the abused pets of the world" thing was a little strange. There were a lot of people who were abused, too. He didn't see anybody paying anyone to find *them* a better home. He felt a quick pinch of anger and ran his fingertips along the bills in his pocket to settle himself down. *Forty bucks, though. Not bad.*

It wouldn't take him long to pull together cash for a bus ticket now. He was going to need some for living expenses, too, until he actually found out where his dad was. Minneapolis was pretty big, and his dad was supposed to be staying at a friend's, but Kurt had never met that friend and didn't even know his name. One thing he did know: his dad might be able to use some extra money, at least enough to get them both set up somewhere. Kurt added that to the expense list in his mind.

A rectangle of paper lay in his path. Kurt stopped and bent down to pick it up. "Reward," it said. But the blurry photo wasn't the one of the calico. It was a picture of Penny. Kurt let the paper drop from his fingers as if it had bit him, and made a right onto his street.

Like those in the rest of the small houses on the block, the windows of his grandmother's house were dark. Kurt breathed a relieved sigh as he silently approached the front door. He turned the handle, but the deadbolt kept the door shut fast. Kurt stepped back off the porch and looked up in time to see a meteor streak across the sky.

He suddenly remembered his mother's voice: "*Make a wish.*" A memory surfaced of a hand wiping the hair off his forehead. But the memory was soon quashed as he thought of how the drugs had taken that soft voice and made it into something older—and hard. The second memory made the burn scars on the inside of his forearm itch, and Kurt scratched them absently.

Making his way to the side of the house, he found the crowbar he left stashed beneath his bedroom window for the times when he found the door locked. Two pops with the bar, and his window was open. He placed the crowbar back in the bushes, then hoisted himself up and over the windowsill. It had been easy for him to take the latch off his window. *But then again*, thought Kurt with both an inward wince and a grimace of cold satisfaction, *I've always been good with tools.*

He switched on the bedside lamp and sat listening to the silence of the house for a moment before reaching over to the small table beside him. He picked up a smooth, cool object. It could easily be dismissed as an ordinary rock, but closer inspection revealed the swirling grain that covered its surface. Petrified wood. Kurt's father had given it to him when he'd left him here. His dad said that he'd found the rock when he was Kurt's age. He explained that the original scrap of wood had fallen to the ground long ago and after untold years of water running over, under, and through it, only mineral deposits remained, turning it to stone. Kurt hadn't wanted to take it. All he'd wanted was to go with his dad instead of being left with his grandmother, someone he saw only once a year at most.

But his dad said that Kurt needed a real home and that until he could find steady work and an apartment for them, Kurt would have to stay with his grandmother. Even though Kurt insisted it didn't matter where they lived, his dad shook his head and then pressed the piece of petrified wood into his palm.

"Listen," his father said, forcing Kurt to look in his eyes, "life runs through you and takes things away. But in time, what it leaves behind is stronger than before."

Now, sitting in his room, Kurt squeezed the piece of petrified wood. He knew his dad wanted him to be as strong as that rock, but instead he felt like there was a rock in his chest, cold and hard.

Kurt put the stone back on the end table, pulled off his clothes, and turned off the lamp. He lay in the dark, thinking of all the things that had been taken from him. It was time, he thought, that he got something back.

Carrie had returned to the comfort of the easy chair. Mavis stuck her long nose close to her hand and asked, "Are you sure this is a good idea?"

Carl walked over to stand in front of her chair. "We wouldn't be dealing with all of this if you hadn't gotten yourself in a wad again, Carrie."

"You don't know what you're talking about, Carl," Carrie snapped.

Carl blinked and said nothing.

"I'm hungry," said Penny.

"Not now." Carrie could feel her voice getting tight and the beginnings of a hornet's nest in her chest. She ran her fingers five times through her hair to quiet the buzzing in her ears.

"The other people fed me whenever I wanted to eat," pouted the dachshund.

Carrie looked over and studied Penny's plump form. "Well, it wasn't good for you."

"But it *felt* good," insisted Penny.

"Feeling good and what's good for you are two entirely different things." Carrie stood up. Moving always helped when she started to get this way. "It's about time you learned that."

Will's Blog: I ran again. Just wanted to make sure that I could do it a couple of days in a row without dying. I'm worried about running with Claire. I've seen her. She's fast. And I know it sounds dumb, but she kind of reminds me of a gazelle. I know I'm no gazelle, but I want to make sure that at least I'm no water buffalo, either.

I was practically dying on that last, lung-exploding

mile home. I would have barfed if I'd had anything in my stomach. The birds were really loud, too. It must have been because of the sunrise. I can see how people think they sound nice, but it would have been a lot nicer if it hadn't been so early. Too bad the word *bird* is the taste of buttered bread; I've always liked it.

Kurt's eyes opened as the first rays of sunlight fell across his pillow. He lay there and listened to the birds in the yard. They sounded pretty. After a moment, he got up and pulled jeans up over his boxers. He picked up the tee shirt he'd worn the day before, but threw it in the corner after giving the pits a sniff. His grandmother was cool about washing his stuff, he thought, as he grabbed another shirt from the top of a neatly folded stack of clothes on his dresser. She was actually pretty cool about a lot of things.

His grandmother was already up and starting a pot of coffee when Kurt walked into the kitchen. She said good morning, and Kurt saw that she hadn't yet put in her false teeth.

Fang. Fangs. Fangless, he thought, as he reached past her for a box of Pop-Tarts.

"Teeth?" he said, not looking directly at her, not wanting to see the lines of pink gums again.

She laughed. "Just taking a break." But she padded down the hall anyway, to retrieve her dentures from her bedroom. Kurt had seen them there before, on her nightstand, like some white and pink plastic guard dog—minus the rest of the dog. Thinking of the guard dog made him remember Mavis and then everything else from the night before. He dipped his hand briefly into his pocket to make sure the folded bills were still there.

Kurt was pulling his Pop-Tart from the toaster and juggling the hot pastry back and forth between his hands when his grandmother came back into the kitchen.

"Kurt, get a plate," she said.

"No need," he answered. He took a first bite and chewed with his mouth open to allow the heat to escape.

"Can I call my dad today?" he asked through another bite.

"I think he moved again, honey," said his grandmother. She didn't look at him as she poured herself a cup of the strong-smelling coffee. "And I don't know if he has a phone yet. He'll let us know when he does."

"Is he in his own place now?" His dad had promised that this whole separation thing was just until he got a new job and an apartment.

"Yes, I think he is," she replied. "But you know, he wants you to finish the school year before he comes to get you." Kurt made a face. "Give it another few weeks." She picked up a pack of cigarettes and shook one out. "Anyway, your old Gram likes the company. She's not letting you run off so fast." She felt around in the pocket of her bathrobe, drew out a plastic lighter, and gave it a couple of flameless flicks.

"These sure don't last long," she said.

Kurt put his hand in his own pocket and pulled out the lighter he'd lifted at the store. Again, his fingers brushed against the folded bills.

"Here you go, Grandma," he said. He handed her the yellow lighter. "I found this one on my way home yesterday."

"Thank you, honey." His grandmother gave him a peck on the cheek before popping the cigarette between her lips and lighting it. Kurt watched as she drew the smoke in and exhaled it through her nose, then took a drink of coffee. Her face crumpled into a grimace.

"This coffee is bitter this morning. I might as well be drinking sludge." But she took another sip anyway.

"Sure, Grandma," he said. He wasn't sure what he was saying sure to, but he decided it didn't matter.

Kurt went back to his room to get his shoes and stopped back at the bathroom to brush his teeth. Then he grabbed his backpack and yelled a good-bye as he began his walk to school. *My dad has his own place now*. Kurt liked his grandmother all right, but there was no way he was going to stay in this hole of a town for the rest of the school year. He had forty bucks in his pocket and a way to get more—a lot more. It wouldn't be long before he was out of here. *Cool*.

The birds kept up their racket as he walked to school. He liked it. They sounded so pretty.

"Breakfast!" called Carrie. She rapped a spoon against the side of the cat food can and yelled again. "Time to eat!"

The cat door swung open as Belle slipped into the kitchen.

"Where are the other two?" Carrie asked when the orange tabby and the little black-and-white cat didn't appear. But Belle didn't answer.

"Gone," said Carl, coming in from the living room. His tail twitched in irritation as he stared at the unopened cat food can in Carrie's hand. Mavis and Penny, too, were waiting expectantly at their bowls.

"Gone." Carl impatiently repeated the word. "Last night. The tabby said, and I quote, 'he wasn't changing his name for nobody, and he wasn't sharing no house with no stinkin' dogs.'" Carl's lip seemed to lift up into a sneer at that last tidbit of information, but Mavis's and Penny's attentive gazes were still glued to the can of food.

"What about the little one?" asked Carrie, worried now. The anxiety seemed to take root at the base of her skull. She felt it crawl up and over to her forehead, where it lodged in the creases there. She slapped it, startling Carl. "She's much too young to be out on her own."

"She left with the orange guy," said Carl. "She's *fine*, Carrie. *We're* the ones that are starving."

"I'm hungry. I'm hungry. I'm hungry. I'm hungry." Penny began to spin around and around in frustration.

Mavis lunged and gave the dachshund a nip on the ear. Penny shrieked.

"Shut up! Shut up! Shut up!" snarled Mavis. Belle leapt out of the way of the bickering dogs.

"Better feed us now, Carrie," said Carl, stepping clear of the fray as well. "It's getting ugly down here."

"Sorry," said Carrie. She opened the cans and filled the bowls. The worry over the escaped cats made her forehead itch. She slapped at it again as she listened to the kitchen fill with gulping sounds as the others inhaled their breakfast.

Will's Blog: I actually had a real conversation with Claire as I was heading into the library. So that's why I'm sitting here in front of a monitor, talking to myself, instead of eating, even though I'm starving after running this morning.

I can't believe I was so nervous while I was talking to her. It almost seemed like she was waiting for me to say something to her. Could that be possible? If she thought about me even a fraction of the time I think about her, then I'd be happy. Because that would still be a lot.

She was wearing running clothes, which at least gave me an opening, so I asked her to go for a run with me. She said yes! And she said it like it wasn't a big deal or anything. She didn't even seem to have to think about it. That's good, right?

"When?" she asked me. For the first time, I noticed that she has just a few really light freckles across the tops of her cheeks. How can freckles look so good?

"I don't know. Tomorrow?" Even though by now I was so hungry that the tomato taste of the word *tomorrow* almost made me drool and despite the fact that my legs felt as dead as two telephone poles after my run this morning, I wanted to say, "Now, later, tomorrow, forever." Good thing I talk to myself inside my head and not out loud. If anyone knew the things I *didn't* say, they'd probably lock me up in a place worse than where my brother is.

"Okay, we'll do something tomorrow."

Yeah. She said "do something tomorrow." Not just running, but *something*. What does that mean? But I didn't get a chance to say anything more than okay, because that's when her cousin showed up. Lydia? I think that's her name. I wasn't paying all that much attention to her. I think she's the same age as Claire, but that's as far as the similarities go. For one thing, this chick has a kid. Noah, I think she called him. At first, I thought she must be watching him or something. But he's hers, and somebody other than her should be watching him, or they should at least clean him up or something.

Well, that was the end of Claire paying any attention to me, because she got all mushy and started to babble baby talk. And then she picked him up and kissed him, even though his face looked all sticky and his feet were dirty and grubby. Ugh, *grubby*. I wish that wasn't the word I'd thought of just then. I don't think that I need to explain by now that it's another one that tastes totally vile.

So anyway, I'm really not that into little kids. Can you tell?

Claire's cousin isn't all that bad-looking. She does have good hair, long and blonde, but she just looked kind of, I don't know, old. I've seen that old look before. My mother had it for as long as I can remember. Those years of always saying how sick she felt, and then when she actually became sick, it made her look like that. Let's just say that chemo wasn't exactly her fountain of youth.

My brother got that used-up look, too. It started with too many cigarettes and beers and then too many months of sitting on the living room couch with his bong. And then, finally, after the stretches of not sleeping when he ditched everything for meth, he really looked bad. Better living through chemistry? Not so true, as far as my family goes.

Yeah, anything about Claire's cousin that might look okay evaporated because she seemed so old and used up. Plus she reeked of smoke. And when I looked at that baby's fuzzy hair with little flecks of ash mixed in, I thought, whoa, who does that? First of all, who smokes around a baby, anyway? And second, who drops ashes on their freaking baby's head?

The freaking word *freaking* tastes like black licorice. Black ashes, black licorice? It'd be bad enough to have candy stuck in a baby's hair, but cigarette ashes? That is so not okay.

Good thing she had to go. Then I at least got to talk to Claire for a couple of minutes alone again before she had to leave, too. She said she'd see me later. I can hardly wait for later. I watched her run off. She looks so great. Shorts are a good thing. And now, *later* doesn't seem too bad, either.

I can't believe that lunch is almost over. No time left to eat now, but spending the time with Claire was totally worth it. Next, I meet with that Kurt kid. Creep. I've already decided not to say anything to him about the lighter or the flyer. Why should I care, anyway? It's not like it's my job to care about him.

Kurt sat with his arms crossed as the senior explained all the red marks on the paper he was handing to him, but he wasn't really listening. He was thinking about after school. He looked up at the clock above the door and saw that he still had 15 minutes left with this guy. *Fifteen minutes of hell, boring hell.* Kurt wished he could somehow make the clock hands move faster.

"Does that make sense?" Will asked.

"What?" Kurt straightened in his seat a bit, hoping to figure out what Will was asking him.

"This." Will pointed to an area on the sheet that was circled in red. "Do you think you can fix this?" He furrowed his brow at him and pointed again.

"Yeah." Kurt took the paper without reading any of the red ink comments, then re-crossed his arms. *Yeah, right.*

There was a long moment of silence.

You think because you're older than me, and bigger, that I have to sit here and listen to you pretend to be my teacher or something?

"Do you have the new assign—I mean, the paper finished?" Will finally broke the silence.

Sure, zombie. Kurt reached into his backpack and handed over a few loose sheets. *Here's your assignment, jerk.*

"Do you think there's any way you could do this on a computer?" Will asked as he shuffled through the papers. "I mean, if you don't have one at home, maybe you can do it here after school."

"I work," Kurt interrupted. "I don't have time to use the computer for my *assignments.*"

They sat in silence again for a minute. Kurt couldn't tell what his tutor was thinking about, only that he had a really strange expression on his face. *He looks like he just tasted something rotten.*

"Okay," Will spoke as he looked up at the clock, too. "It's early, but I guess you can go."

Without another word, Kurt grabbed his backpack and was out the door.

He left school to head in a direction opposite his grandmother's house. As usual, he shunned the loud groups of students heading to their cars or hopping on their skateboards, the buses, or whatever as they celebrated the end of another day of classes. *They sound like a bunch of stupid chickens*, he thought. *Except chickens sound smarter*, he decided. He walked faster, away from the noise.

Carrie had said she'd meet him at the mini-mart at the edge of downtown at four-thirty. That gave him a good 45 minutes to get somewhere that was only a 10-minute walk. He slowed as he neared the city park, to observe a small black dog running madly, barking in short, sharp yips at a group of little kids. The dog's curly coat bounced as it leapt in the air.

Hey, that dog's not on a leash, he thought. This was just the kind of thing Carrie had told him to keep an eye out for. If an owner didn't think to keep their dog on a leash, they obviously didn't care about it enough. An unleashed dog could run off, get lost, or end up beneath the tires of a car. Carrie'd assured him that any animals he found in this kind of situation would be way better off with her. Kurt didn't know about that, but he really didn't care, either. What he did know was that the little black dog could be worth another quick forty bucks.

The dog suddenly left the screams and shrieks of the laughing kids to make a beeline toward a squirrel. The squirrel first headed one way, then doubled back to race within 10 feet of Kurt's sneakers and right across the street. The dog had nearly caught up with it and was only inches from the squirrel's flying tail.

Kurt heard the horn and the skid of tires before he ever saw the SUV. The dog froze in front of the stopped car, and Kurt's heart made a sideways lurch before it resumed a steady, but faster beat.

"Buddy!" A woman's frightened voice cut through the park. "Buddy, come!" The little black dog finally moved out of its terrified statue stance and whirled around to race back to the playground, where its owner waited for him. The squirrel set up a scolding tirade from its perch in a maple tree. After another, longer honk at the departing dog from the exasperated SUV driver, the vehicle drove off.

Kurt turned toward the playground, where he saw a lady bend down to scoop the dog into her arms. He felt a bolt of anger at her for letting her dog scare him like that, and he was starting to get what Carrie was talking about. Maybe she was right after all. He didn't want to see the dog hit by the car, and it had been a very close call.

He directed his thoughts to the retreating forms of the woman and the dog. *Okay, Buddy. You're first.* He tipped his head and looked at the sky, hoping the sparkles he saw in the air would calm his racing heart a little. He counted to 10 as he watched the tiny lights dance and felt his breathing slow back to almost normal.

Kurt's hands were still a little shaky as he reached into

the side pouch of his backpack to rummage for his only smoke. It was bent, but not broken. *Good.* He stuck it between his lips and resumed his walk toward the mini-mart, but stopped when he remembered giving the lighter to his grandmother. *Stupid!* Now he'd have to wait until he reached the mini-mart to get a light. Taking the cigarette out of his mouth, he noticed a girl pushing a stroller toward him. She had long blonde hair and an okay face, but the rest of her looked pretty good. She appeared to be only a couple of years older than he was, but those couple of years were enough to put her completely out of his reach. She stopped for a moment and lit a cigarette. *Bingo*, thought Kurt. He reached her in a few long strides. "Cute baby," he said, looking at the yellow-haired infant. Kurt raised his head to look at the girl. "Got a light?" he asked. Ten seconds later, he was on his way to meet Carrie.

Carrie tapped a beat on the steering wheel with her fingertips, absorbed with thoughts of the two wayward cats. She'd caught them once, but it might be a lot harder to lure them a second time. Then she thought of Kurt and smiled. They didn't know him. That was the beautiful part of the plan.

She slowed the car at the sight of something dead on the side of the road. A closer look confirmed her suspicion and fear. The tangle of blood and black-and-white fur was the little cat. Carrie sighed in frustration as she pulled over and got out to open her trunk. Grabbing a towel, she walked back around the car to gently wrap up the body and then placed it in the trunk beside her spare tire. She closed the lid and then quickly scanned the area for the orange tabby. Finding nothing else, she got back in the car and put it in gear.

She checked her rearview mirror to see whether her lane was clear, shaking her head at her own reflection. *They just don't know what's good for them. It'd all work out perfectly if they'd just follow my plan.* Carrie resumed her tapping beat on the steering wheel, then pulled back onto the pavement and drove toward town.

Kurt settled into the car and clicked his seat belt into place. Carrie sniffed the air. "Smoking will kill you," she said.

"My grandmother smokes," Kurt answered, long deafened to lectures on the evils of tobacco. "And she's pretty old."

Carrie shrugged. "Lucky maybe, or else the big C just hasn't caught up with her yet." She didn't look at him, but stared straight out the windshield. "Both my parents passed away before I really had a chance to grow up. I wasn't ready at all when they went. They died 10 months apart." She was quiet for a moment. "And they both smoked like chimneys. They never listened to me, and look what happened to them—they died."

Kurt didn't know what to say to that, so instead he told her about the black dog in the park. Carrie nodded. "I've seen that dog around before, and it's *never* on a leash." She turned the corner and headed onto the highway entrance ramp.

"Where are we going?" Kurt asked, suddenly realizing he'd never even thought about it.

"We need to go to the mall," Carrie replied. "You're going to need some equipment to do this right."

They left the enormous pet warehouse, loaded down with supplies, and Kurt shoved the soft-sided vinyl pet carrier, the plastic bags of dog treats, and the catnip into his backpack. As he jammed it all in, his long sleeve moved up and over his elbow. As he withdrew his hand, Carrie grabbed the hem of his sleeve, further exposing the inside of his arm. Kurt knew that now she could see the line of round burns marching up his arm to the crook of his elbow.

Kurt yanked his arm back, and she let go. "Who's mistreating you?" she demanded.

"No one," Kurt answered, his neck growing hot as red anger and embarrassment collided. He shoved the anger and humiliation back down and away, hidden where they belonged.

"It's getting late, and I gotta get going. My grandmother's going to start wondering where I am."

"Did your grandmother do this to you?"

Kurt turned a disdainful face toward Carrie. "My grandmother *takes care* of me." And then in a quiet, level voice, he added, "And I took care of the person who did it." Kurt felt a muscle jump in his cheek at the thought of that person.

Carrie looked away. "If you ever want to talk," she said, getting in the car, "I'm a good listener."

Kurt said nothing more, and when she dropped him off, he ran as fast as he could through the warm, early evening breeze to his grandmother's house. He found her on the front porch, with smoke wreathing her gray head of hair. For a minute, he let himself enjoy being glad to see her. "Smoking's bad for you," he panted.

His grandmother nodded. "Don't I know it. But so is fast food, and I'm hungry for a burger and some greasy fries. What do you say?"

Will's Blog: I was not going to open another can of something for dinner. Cooking isn't something I spend too much time thinking about, and as long as it's food, most of the time whatever plops out of a can is dinner to me. I'm not really complaining, and there sure isn't anyone else here to do it for me, either.

I was completely starved when I got home. So I slammed the last bits of chips from the bottom of the bag, washing them down with about half the carton of milk right from the refrigerator before I even put my school stuff down on the kitchen chair. I was still hungry, but like I said, I wasn't opening any more cans.

I haven't been to the burger place for a while. I don't like to spend too much money on fast food. I know that I have some money, but that's put away for school. I have the house, too. I could sell it, I guess. I don't know. At least my mom did *that* for me. As soon as I turned 18, she put me down in her will to get everything—her insurance, the house, the car. She knew that if my brother got his hands on anything, it'd be gone in a week. And that would be one really bad week.

So this time, I let myself go out to eat. I ordered a couple of cheeseburgers right off. Why pretend that I'm going to eat only one and then have to go back and order—and wait for—the other one? The fries there are great, and the milkshakes are even better. I get vanilla every time. I always think about ordering a different flavor, but I never do. Maybe I'm just a vanilla kind of guy.

You know who's not a vanilla person? My brother. But neither's that Kurt kid. Anyway, all I wanted to do was eat my food, and in he comes with some old lady. It's bad enough that I had to look at his—what would be a good way to describe it—sullen, maybe, or, better yet, feral face at school today. *Feral*. Yeah, like those pinch-faced cats that hang out behind the dumpsters at the convenience store.

Actually, the old lady didn't look that much older than my mom. Has the same gray hair and the same kind of potato-shaped body. There must be a store around here somewhere that sells nothing but those flowered blouses and thick polyester pants that old ladies always seem to wear. But even from the booth where I was sitting, I heard him call her Grandma.

So here's what I can't figure out. Why did I think it was a good idea to go up to the counter where they were standing? I don't even *like* that kid. Why did I have to say hi and get nothing back but a look? Why did I have to stick out my big stupid hand when his grandmother introduced herself, saying to call her Agnes?

And worst of all, why did I have to ask him what kind of milkshake he was ordering? Chocolate banana caramel, he said, and then looked at me like he knew what a total nothing I was. I knew then how completely vanilla I really am. But I don't want that. Am I doomed to stay this way, or will something finally happen to make me into more than I am? Maybe it'll be Claire. Maybe having someone like her around, someone who might actually like me, will change things. But what if it doesn't?

As I type, the tastes of the words swirl in my mouth. But as always, they're empty, never filling.

"It's so sad," sighed Penny as Carrie dug the shovel into the earth. Mavis said nothing as she lay down and put her nose on her front paws, settling a mournful gaze on the towel-wrapped bundle.

"I should have stopped them. I should have told you," Carl fretted. He limped back and forth beside Carrie's legs.

"It's not your fault, Carl," Carrie said, a little out of breath from shoveling. But the activity quieted the whisperings in her head that had been bothering her all evening. "They wouldn't have listened to you, anyway. Now, move out of the way before I accidentally bean you." Carl hopped away.

She finished the hole and then put the little cat's body down inside. It seemed to weigh no more than the towel itself, and she filled the hole back up with the softened dirt. "Now, where is that marker?" she asked no one in particular. Her eyes fell upon the small wooden cross that lay on the grass a few feet away from her. She pushed it into the newly covered grave, and then the four of them turned to head back toward the house, leaving the rows of small wooden crosses behind them.

The same as the day before, the playground was alive with activity when Kurt arrived. The high-pitched squeals of the children rose up around his ears like the buzz of a billion insects. Only looking up and focusing on the flashes of light against the blue sky kept him from screaming back. It was really getting to him today. Too much like the screams he'd heard at the worst times, when he'd had to fight the urge to push his dresser in front of his bedroom door to keep it all out. Too much like when he'd force himself to actually go out there and try to make Mark stop.

Most of the time it had worked when he would scream "Stop!" Mark would storm off, his huge truck spitting gravel into the yard when he peeled out. His mom would let him put an ice pack on her eye or jaw. Then, at least for a little while, it would be quiet and they'd watch a TV show together. But even in the midst of how good it was to spend time alone with her, it always felt so bad, too. It was like he had to pay some sort of awful admission to get to the good parts. He'd always hated feeling that way and wished that the feeling would leave, along with Mark and his truck.

Kurt kicked a stone across the sunbaked sidewalk before him, staving off the boredom of waiting and trying not to look like—*what? A perv? A freak?* He was well aware of the weight of the backpack and the vinyl animal carrier inside it. He stopped kicking for a minute to pull out the carrier.

Am I a freak? he wondered. No, he decided. *That Will guy is a freak. Jeez, he was practically hitting on my grandmother at the drive-in.* At least he'd let Kurt go early yesterday, but still, he was some kind of stalker freak. The word *stalker* made him self-conscious about why he was in the park. *Buddy, you good little dog, you're all mine today.*

He'd been waiting a good half hour now, but there was no sign of Buddy. Kurt was already starting to think about bagging the whole thing for the day when he saw the cigarette blonde from the day before. The stroller was gone, and she now carried the fluffy-haired baby like a sack of rocks under her arm. Kurt patted himself down in the vain hope of a forgotten butt. *Nothing.* The girl sat the baby down in the grass and plopped beside it. Kurt resumed his stone kicking around the perimeter of the park, keeping one eye out for Buddy and the other on the blonde.

Some guys showed up before the dog did. There were three of them, and Kurt had seen them before in town. One had hair down the middle of his back, while the other two had shaved heads. Silver studs and piercings sprouted from their flesh everywhere, and tattoos ranging from elaborate to homemade adorned their skin. Seeing them, Kurt decided to abandon his plan of bumming a cigarette off the chick. Man, if he thought high school kids would cream him, these freaks wouldn't even leave a body.

He maneuvered himself behind a tree and watched as

the biggest guy whisked the baby up off the ground and tossed it into the air. The surprised baby let out a wail, and they all laughed as the baby flew up into the sky again and again. After several trips, the girl reached out her arms to hold the sobbing baby close. Kurt saw the laughter that was still on her face, and he grew cold, despite the heat of the day.

But a different face loomed large in Kurt's mind, one that taunted and laughed at his pain and fear. Mark had always thought it was hilarious to scare him like that, too. Throwing Kurt fully clothed into an algae-slicked pond? To Mark, it was a freaking laugh riot. Taking his hands off the steering wheel of his truck until Kurt was sure they'd go off the road and down the steep embankment? To Mark, it was comedic genius. Call him on it, and Mark would jeer, saying Kurt was a girl, a fairy, and then he would tell his mother it was just a joke.

"It's just his way of playing." That's what his mom would say. But Kurt saw the pleading in her eyes, her nervousness clear as her gaze flitted between him and Mark. Just thinking about it made his scars itch furiously, and he had to shake his head to clear his mind of that hateful image.

The girl sat the crying baby down again and let the long-haired guy light her cigarette. Kurt instantly hated that guy. *I know exactly what you're all about*, Kurt thought.

The girl took a deep drag off her smoke, and Kurt suddenly wanted one, too, and bad.

Just at that moment, a black blur raced past the edge of his vision while a voice called out, "Buddy, come! Buddy, come here!" Kurt gripped the carrier tightly, angry enough now to take everyone's dogs. He watched as Buddy ran a scattered lap pattern through the park, and he saw the woman finally give up chasing the dog, eventually going to sit on a bench with a newspaper in front of her face. She wasn't even watching the dog.

Kurt waited until Buddy got near him, then held a treat just out of the dog's reach. Buddy stepped closer and sniffed, and then Kurt had him in his grasp. Without a sound, he stuffed Buddy into the carrier. He sneaked one last look at the girl and her friends. The baby sat quietly in a blue tobacco cloud. As much as he hated seeing that, all Kurt could think about was how badly he wanted to cop a smoke of his own.

Will's Blog: So instead of running, Claire asked me if I wanted to go to town with her to buy a baby present for her cousin. Is this a date? It is hanging out, I guess. And for once, I wasn't the one doing the asking. Even though shopping for baby stuff isn't exactly on my list of favorite things to do, I'm not going to tell her that. No way, not when, for the first time in months, I was spending time with someone other than myself when I wasn't in school.

Since they took my brother away, I haven't wanted to hang with my friends. What would we talk about, anyway? Not my brother. I mean, I didn't exactly have a list of prison fun facts to pass along. And what could they possibly say about the worst part of it? "Bummer about your mom, dude"?

I wonder if I could ever talk to Claire about what happened. I mean, she knows about it. Everyone in this town *knows*. But she hasn't ever brought it up. And it feels way too good just being normal for a change for me to bring it up.

Anyway, when Claire and I got to the store, we had to go down rows of nothing but pink, blue, and yellow bunnies and big-eyed baby ducks until she finally found what she was looking for—one of those rattle things that babies chew on when they're getting their teeth. I only hope that her cousin keeps it cleaner than that baby's feet.

After that, we were just walking along on the sidewalk and I was thinking I should ask her if she wanted to get something to eat or go to the coffee shop or something, when suddenly, I spotted that Kurt kid about half a block ahead of us.

He was walking fast. I could see his backpack bumping against his body, and he was carrying, what, a purse? It looked weird—that kid doesn't seem like the man-bag type to me.

That's when I did something really stupid. I could hear Claire asking me a question, but instead of answering her, instead of just taking one little second to turn and look at her, I watched Kurt stop at a pole, look at the paper stuck to it, and then walk away even faster. By the time I turned back to look at Claire, she had this sour expression on her face. I could feel myself getting red, and when I asked her to repeat what she'd just said, she replied that it was nothing and said she had to go. Then she left.

I could tell I'd pissed her off. *Stupid. Stupid. Stupid!* I'd totally ignored this fantastic girl who was talking to me, just to stare at some loser kid that I have to tutor. That sour look on her face reminded me of something. You know which word tastes like sour limes? The word *stupid*.

"This is wonderful!" exclaimed Carrie as Kurt gently pulled the little dog from the carrier, then sat him, shivering, on her kitchen floor. "Your first rescue!" She bent down to pick up the little dog and held him next to her ear.

"I'm scared," he whimpered.

"Is Buddy okay?" Kurt asked, concern cutting across his face.

"Buddy, huh? He's just a little confused is all," Carrie reassured him. "He'll need a new name, though."

"He *looks* like a Buddy to me," said Kurt.

"Fine, then." Carrie had no interest in upsetting the boy. She set Buddy down on the floor, and both Mavis and Penny stepped forward to sniff him up and down.

"Stay off my rug," instructed Mavis.

"Yeah," added Penny, "and when I get one, stay off *mine*, too."

Buddy didn't answer, but stood stock still as the two dogs sniffed him. "See," Carrie told Kurt, "they're already getting acquainted."

"What about the woman who owned him? Won't she be—"

Buddy looked anxiously around the kitchen. "Where's Momma? I want Momma!" he whined.

"Forget Momma!" Carrie spat. Carl jumped off the seat of the kitchen chair with a thud, and Kurt swiveled his head to stare at Carrie. "What I meant was, his Momma almost let him get killed." Carrie looked at Kurt with what she hoped was a calmer expression than she actually felt, and she made an effort to try to slow down her words.

Buddy whined again, and Carl hissed back.

"Zip it, Carl," Carrie warned, narrowing her eyes at him. She noticed the concern still etched on Kurt's brow and desperately wanted it to go away.

"You've done a good thing here, Kurt." She took a deep breath. "A very good thing. Buddy, here." She picked Buddy back up and handed him to Kurt. "Buddy is safe now, and this will be a good lesson to that woman. Take care of your animals, or you won't have them anymore." Carrie walked to the kitchen and took two twenties from her purse on the countertop. She held them out to him.

Kurt looked at the dark eyes of the curly-haired dog.

"Are you taking me back to Momma?" Buddy whined, a bit louder this time.

Kurt handed the dog back to Carrie, taking the bills in exchange.

"You should be proud of yourself," said Carrie, stroking Buddy's gleaming black fur. "You're a hero, Kurt. You probably saved his life."

He seemed to brighten at that, she thought. Carrie wished she could understand more about this boy. She was ready to listen, if only he would just talk to her.

~

"You're spending more time out and about. Where have you been keeping yourself?" Kurt's grandmother asked him at the dinner table.

Kurt swallowed his bite of fried baloney sandwich, using the extra time to think of a good answer. "Hanging out" was all he managed. His grandmother looked expectantly at him, waiting for him to elaborate. Kurt shifted in his chair. Collecting spare change from her pockets was one thing. Lying to her was something else altogether. An idea materialized, and he reached into his pocket and pulled out one of the twenties. "Actually, I've been working. Here," he said, laying it next to her plate.

His grandmother looked at the money as if she'd never seen anything like it before. "Working? Doing what?"

"I've been, um, helping this lady out. Helping her with her animals. She has a lot of animals."

She smiled. "You've always had a soft spot for creatures. I remember that kitten you had. . . . " Her voice trailed off as she remembered what had happened to the cat. She seemed to snap back to the subject at hand and asked, "How did you hear about this job?"

Kurt took a long drink of milk and then wiped his lips with his paper napkin. "A flyer," he answered. He pushed the twenty closer to her. "I want you to have this."

"Oh, Kurt, keep your money." His grandmother shook her head.

"I want to help out," said Kurt. He thought again of the coins he'd taken from her and took a breath. "I actually owe you some money, anyway. Um, I borrowed some change from your pockets a couple of times."

His grandmother gave a laugh. "I *thought* my bingo change was getting pretty light, but I decided I was just beginning to forget things"—she raised her eyebrows at him—"old lady that I am."

"You're not that old," said Kurt, thinking he didn't even know how old she really was. He felt a little bad about that, like it somehow meant he didn't care about her.

"Well, I'm glad to see that you're starting to take an interest in things around here," his grandmother began. "I want you to think of this as your home."

"I'm going to go live with my dad," Kurt stated flatly, the warmth he'd felt just a few seconds earlier fleeing back into the shadows. "When is he getting a phone? At least give me his address so I can write him a letter." *Or go see him*, he added silently.

"I don't have it, honey. I wish I did. I miss your dad, too." She paused for a moment. "You got a letter from your mom today."

Kurt froze. "I don't want it. Throw it away."

"I got one, too. She's doing real good there. She says she knows how wrong she was and that she's very sorry." Kurt stared down at the crust of his sandwich, willing the tears that were beginning to float into his eyes to just dry up. He thought of the piece of petrified wood in his room. *Stones don't cry.* He remembered that when he had last talked to his dad, he'd felt like there was a rock in his chest.

He felt that again now, and he was glad. *I'm going to stay hard inside, just like that stone*.

"She wants to try to make it up to you when she gets out," his grandmother said, gently. "I know—and she knows—that what you did wasn't your fault. You were a hero, Kurt."

Kurt got up from the table. The sandwich in his stomach felt like it might make a reappearance, and he carried his plate to the sink. *Twice in one day*, he thought, *I've been called a hero*. He swallowed the sick feeling back down.

"I'm going to live with my dad," he repeated. He went to his room, and a few minutes later, he heard his grandmother slip the envelope under his door.

Will's Blog: I can't believe how much I freaked out about Claire yesterday. I am so damaged. Even my brother would never have done something like that when he was my age. There's no way I would want to be anything like him now or even have anything to do with him. But at least, for a while, the guy was cool. And that's something I'm definitely not.

So I went for a run. I needed to do something to make myself stop thinking, for even a little while. Running works better than anything else I've tried to keep things I don't want from getting into my head. I can't help wondering how everything might be now if my brother'd gone running instead of polluting himself with drugs and booze to escape. I'll never really know, but I bet it would have turned out better. And my mom, too. Not that I would have expected her to run. Man, I can't picture her running for any reason. I mean, even if there were a pack of radioactive zombies after her, she'd probably never even break into a fast walk. But maybe if she'd found something other than her health to obsess about, then . . . But I guess that's just another thing I'll never know.

Anyway, today I saw Claire running right past the baby store. We ran together for a couple of miles on her way home. I'd been kind of worried that she'd kick my—okay, *butt* isn't as bad a taste as the other word I could have used, and if I don't mind the taste of buttermilk, I can use the word *butt* all I want.

So I did okay running with her, not breathing too hard or anything. That's when she told me what she said the last time we were together. Turns out she wasn't mad at me at all. She actually was *embarrassed*. She thought I wasn't listening to her because what she said was too lame to pay any attention to. Can you believe that? A girl like her, worried about what *I* thought?

So then I told her that I'd thought she was mad at me for spacing out on her. And then we both stopped and looked at each other. It took me a couple of seconds to realize that the sound coming out of my mouth was laughter. I can't remember the last time I laughed. I don't watch much television, and yeah, there have been a few videos online that I thought were kind of funny, but really laugh? Anyway, we both started cracking up, which made it kind of hard to start running again. So we walked the last few blocks to her house.

And the thing I didn't hear her ask was if I wanted to

come to the baby shower for her cousin, which was going to be at Claire's house. It was supposed to be starting right at that time. I wouldn't be able to go home and change or anything, but she said it didn't matter.

I said yes. Of course I said yes. Sorry, but spending time with a girl, especially a girl like Claire, even at some boring baby shower, is way better than talking to myself at home. And here's where she was the coolest. She didn't go off and leave me there while she changed out of her running clothes. She stayed all sweaty, too, so I wouldn't feel weird.

Seeing her there, with her mom and her dad and her whole family, made me the happiest I'd been for a long time. But you know what? At the same time, I've never felt more alone.

No, wait. Why would I even be writing that? Maybe the reason I feel so alone is because I deserve it. I am nothing but a whiner and a complainer—a big, fat baby. My brother called me those things all the time, even before he got so bad.

And you want to know the truth? I *was* a whining baby.

After our dad left, which was in the middle of third grade–is January 6 the middle? It was right after Christmas vacation ended. And when I got home from school that day, the first thing I noticed was the Christmas tree in our front yard. That wouldn't have been weird at all, because it was time to take it down. But what made this year completely different was that all the ornaments were still on it. Then my brother came running out of the garage, carrying the gasoline can and yelling about something. Our mom's shouts didn't make much sense, either, and all I could do was stand there while my brother doused the tree and then threw a match on it. It wasn't until after I heard the whoosh of the fireball that I realized all the presents were going up in flames, too.

Our mom had just told him that our dad was gone, this time for good. He had another family to live with, and another job. I shouldn't have even wanted his stupid presents, but I did. So I asked my mom if I could get another model to build, and it didn't have to be the same one my dad had gotten me. And after I bugged her about it all the time, she finally called me a whiner, too.

So isn't that what I'm doing here, too? Whining? Complaining? I was just at Claire's house. She hardly left me alone for a second. She even walked me halfway home. But instead of thinking and writing about that, I'm going on about something that happened 10 years ago—and tasting it, too. Just typing out the word for that December 25 holiday makes me have to drink a huge glass of water, to wash the taste of gasoline out of my mouth. I guess I'll have to live with those two things being tied together forever.

Buddy finally napped, curled up like a comma next to Penny's warm body. Carrie rubbed her eyes. The little dog's whining had given her the mother of all headaches, and both Belle and Carl had taken off through the cat door to escape the noise. Mavis stepped over to Carrie and pushed her long nose under Carrie's palm.

"Carrie?" she asked, her brow patches knitted over her warm brown eyes.

"It's okay, Mavis. I'm *okay*, Mavis," Carrie added, when the dog would not break her questioning gaze. "My eyes are just tired, is all."

"Why don't you go lie down?" Mavis gave Carrie a nudge toward her bedroom.

But Carrie knew that sleep was not an option.

"I'd really rather make myself a cup of tea," Carrie sighed.

"That's good. You like tea." The German shepherd lay down next to her feet.

"Oh, Mavis." Carrie was suddenly overcome with love for the big dog. She bent down and ran her hand over the big triangle of a head, remembering to give a scratch just under the collar. "You are my best and truest friend. If I didn't have you, who would I talk to?"

"Carl?" Amusement shone from Mavis's bright eyes.

Carrie gave a sigh. "I love him, but Lord, he can be such a pill."

A minute later, Mavis gave a huge dog sigh of her own, asleep now after all the caresses. Carrie thought about getting her tea or checking on Carl and Belle, but instead she lowered herself to the floor and sat next to Mavis, wrapping her arms around the big dog's neck, grateful for a moment of peace.

Kurt sat on his bed with his eyes closed, the letter in his hands. *I'm not going to read it. I don't want to hear any-*

thing she wants to say, he told himself. But still, he had gotten up to retrieve the envelope, carried it back to the bed, and now he opened it and read

Dear Kurt,

I know you probably don't want to hear from me, but I'm going to write anyway. Maybe you won't even read this letter. Maybe you'll throw it away. I know a lot of stuff has gone down for you, and I want you to know how sorry I am. Not that it makes any difference now, I guess, but I still want to let you know that.

Kurt rolled his eyes at that line. *She's right. It doesn't make any difference at all. She could have stopped it by kicking Mark out. Why didn't she?* That was the question he never would let himself ask her. His mom, even at her sickest, had always been nice to him. But letting Mark stay and make their lives hell wasn't nice. After everything that had happened, it actually felt like the meanest part of all.

Unexpectedly, a tear dropped and splashed a runny blob onto the handwriting. He swiped at his eyes with the back of his hand and continued reading.

I'm learning a lot here. It's real hard, but there's nothing to fight the boredom with except hard work, so that's what I'm doing. Group sessions are the toughest. I have to tell everyone what I've done, what I did to you, what I let Mark do to you. I know that the drugs didn't help me make good decisions, but I'm learning that I was still responsible for what happened.

IT WAS NOT YOUR FAULT.

Kurt put the letter down at this point and picked up the piece of petrified wood, squeezing it hard. How did that saying go? You can't get blood from a stone? Well, Mark had gotten blood from him, from a smack in his face, from a tooth knocked loose, from a gusher of a nosebleed, and, that last day, from the cigarette. . . . In the end, though, he had taken all that blood back—and more. He put the rock back in its place on the table.

Your grandmother writes me that you're doing fine and I can try to write to you. I have no right to expect anything from her, either, but she's always been good to me. My lawyer told me that after this, I'll be in the clear. He assured me that no charges were ever filed against you, so I guess I have that to be thankful for, too.

The last line of the letter made Kurt lean back and close his eyes.

I love you with all my heart, and wait for the day when I can see you again.
Love,
Mom

Kurt thought about crumpling the sheet of paper and tossing it in the trash, but he stopped himself. Instead, he got up and opened his bedroom door a crack and listened to see whether his grandmother was still up. He didn't hear anything, and all the lights were out. It was unbearable to just lie there in his room, alone and thinking. So Kurt opened his window and slipped out into the night.

The streets were quiet, and Kurt was grateful not to run into anyone else out for an evening walk. He headed toward town with no particular destination in mind, wanting only to move his arms and legs and to dislodge any remaining thoughts about his mom. He turned down the main street, passing the bright neon colors of the fast-food joint's sign. And then he saw her, the same blonde, there with her baby parked beside her.

This time, the baby stroller was bigger and fancier than the one he'd seen before. It looked brand-new. That guy he couldn't stand, from that day at the park, was there, too. When Kurt walked by, they didn't look up. With their cigarettes, conversation, and loud laughter, they didn't seem to be paying much attention to that baby, either. The neon glow was reflected by the sleeping baby's face.

Even my mom gave me a bedtime, Kurt thought. And the sight of the smoke surrounding the stroller, the girl, and her friend suddenly made the idea of ever smoking a completely unappealing one. The gray, wispy tendrils wafting upward looked so dirty in the glare of the restaurant's lights.

Not wanting to think any more about the smoke or the baby, Kurt continued on until he found his steps leading him out of town and down the road to Carrie's house.

The three dogs launched into a storm of barking as Carrie opened her door and looked at Kurt with surprise. "Another one already?" she asked over the din.

The boy shook his head no. First he looked down at his feet and then past her into the living room. "Um, no. I'm sorry. I was just wondering how, you know, how Buddy was doing." He brushed his hair off his forehead.

"Come on in," she said, pretty sure that it wasn't only concern for the little black dog that brought him here. Was Kurt becoming more convinced that she was right—that what the world most needed was to have the least of its creatures better taken care of? She watched, hope catching in her throat, as he walked across the threshold with Buddy jumping alongside him. Penny furiously sniffed his ankles, while Mavis unceremoniously stuck her nose in his crotch.

"Stop that," Carrie reprimanded the dogs as Kurt crossed his hand over the front of himself. But then he bent down to let the big dog give his cheek a dignified lick. Kurt carefully scratched Mavis's cheek and smiled when the shepherd's tail swept back and forth.

"Is he here to take me back to Momma?" Buddy asked, whirling in excitement.

"Kurt is just here to visit you," Carrie corrected, certain it was about so much more than that. "Isn't that right, Kurt?"

Kurt straightened up. "You really think his old home was that bad?"

Carrie frowned at his question. He shouldn't have asked that. They had already been through this. "A good home," Carrie began, hoping that he got it this time, "is a place of love and safety. My parents, for example, made a wonderful home for me. They made sure all my needs were met. They made sure that nothing bad would ever happen to me."

She paused, confused, unsure how she had gotten on this track. Sadness flowed over her. *I wish they could have made sure nothing bad would ever happen to them.* She forced the image of her parents from her mind.

"So how about you, Kurt? Do you have a good home?"

Kurt nodded, but he didn't look at her. Instead, he did his best to pet three eager dogs with only two hands. "I guess," he replied. "My grandmother's okay. She's real nice to me. She doesn't even have to be; I mean, I'm not her real kid or anything."

"What about your parents? I'm supposing you were *someone's* real kid once."

The boy shrugged.

"That bad, huh?" Carrie thought of the burns she'd seen on his arm.

Kurt brushed the dog hair off his hands and pant legs. "I'm just staying with my grandmother for a while. I'm leaving soon, anyway. I'm going to be living with my dad."

Mavis went to the front door and whined softly to go out. Carrie considered letting them all go into the yard. Penny would stick around, but Buddy was still a wild card. She didn't want a repeat of the burial of earlier that day. She'd have to go outside with them.

"I have to take the dogs out," she told Kurt. "Want to come along?"

Kurt shrugged again, but he followed them all to the

door. The dogs jostled for position. "I'm first," Mavis reminded the smaller dogs with a snarl.

"Calm down, Mavis. You all get to go out." At the word *go*, Carrie opened the door and the animals raced out into the yard. "Our turn," Carrie smiled at Kurt, and they went out under the sparkling stars.

"What about your mother?" Carrie could see the boy's shoulders lift up and drop in the moonlight. The dogs had run up and around to the back of the house, and she could make out their three distinct voices. "Mavis and Penny are arguing about who smelled the raccoon first." Carrie laughed. "But Buddy insists it's a monster."

The boy shot her a look that worried her. What did that look mean?

"So who do *you* talk to?" Carrie asked quickly, trying to change his mood. Her steady pace was taking them up over a small rise, and she noticed that the boy was having trouble keeping up. Didn't young people exercise anymore?

"Nobody. Well, to my grandmother, sometimes."

"Well, you're talking to me."

The boy didn't answer, and they found the dogs busily sniffing the grass around the rows of wooden crosses.

"What is all this?" Kurt asked, sounding uneasy.

"This is where I sometimes come to talk." Carrie smiled softly to herself. "They're some of the best listeners around."

Mavis came bounding up. "Carrie, please tell Penny that I'm the boss."

"Penny," called Carrie. The dachshund waddled up, too, then threw herself down, panting, on the grass. "Penny, mind Mavis." Penny was too out of breath to answer. Carrie looked around anxiously for the little black dog, and Buddy came racing out of the dark after his new companions.

"This was my first dog," Carrie pointed to the cross on the far left side of the rows. "Digger. Well named, too." She enjoyed telling this boy about the various dogs, cats, fish, hamsters, and parakeets who now rested beneath the earth. When she came to the fresh grave, she merely said "stray" and left it at that.

"I wish my parents were here, too," Carrie continued. "I still have so much to tell them. But I need to drive all the way to the cemetery out on the old highway to see them."

"I know someone who died."

The boy's voice startled Carrie from her thoughts. "Who was that?" she asked.

He had shrugging down to an art form. "Just this guy."

"It's time to go back in," Carrie announced, when the boy said nothing more. She rounded up the dogs, and they walked back to the house.

"You seem to have experience with both a good home and a not-so-good one," Carrie said as they reached the front porch. "So who better than you to make sure that animals needing help are taken care of?" She watched closely for his response. She needed a sign that he understood the full meaning of her words.

Kurt nodded slowly at that, which pleased her. And after refusing her offer of a lift home, he headed out the door and back into the night.

~

Will's Blog: I was dreading talking to Kurt today. His paper was a mess, and I ran out of ways to say "This is wrong, wrong, wrong." I was getting depressed, seeing all the red marks on his paper.

When it was time, and he walked through the door, I knew he wasn't going to make this any easier, and a part of me wanted to tell him to just take his wreck of a paper and get out. Man, just one look at him and I could tell how much this kid hates me. That's not my problem, but trying to get his grade up is.

I would have much rather been talking to Claire, even in a room full of people I don't know. Her mom was really nice to me at that baby shower. I was a little weirded out at being there, and I was worried that people might be looking at me but thinking about my brother. Claire's mom never brought that up, though, and she made sure I got a glass of water right away because she said I looked thirsty after my run.

Claire's dad talked to me, too, mostly about school and where I was thinking of going to college. And when he shook my hand, that kind of weirded me out, too. I haven't actually touched another human being since I held my mom, right there on the floor of the grocery store. I hadn't really given that any thought until he grabbed my hand and it felt almost like an electric shock. Like I said, it was weird.

They didn't have to be nice to me. But they were—all of them. And even though they sure didn't have to do it, everyone there talked to me like I was just a regular, normal person. Even though, who am I to them? What do I have? Nothing. A girl, maybe. But that's a *big* maybe. A family? Nope. Friends? Not really. A future? I hope I have one.

At least this Kurt kid has a grandmother. That's more than I have. And if Claire's family can treat me okay, then I guess I can try it, too. To be decent to the kid, I mean. But I'm just not all that big on taking care of people, sorry. After my mom spent all those years demanding it from me, it got pretty old. But like I said, if people as cool as Claire and her family are like that, then maybe I can try it, too. I mean, how hard can it be?

So I looked at the kid again, and this time I saw that he really was just a skinny teenager. Yeah, his hair was pretty long, but even though he wasn't wearing a bunch of logos all over his clothes, he was clean and not some dirtbag. So I ignored his slump and the bored look on his face, and I told him straight out that he needed to do more work on this paper—and on everything, really.

He just shrugged and mumbled something about work and not having enough time.

But I didn't let it bother me this time, and I told him I'd help him—that I was supposed to be helping him.

And that was the first time I can remember that he actually looked at me like I was a real person. And it actually made me *feel* kind of like a real person, like I mattered.

It got better after that. At least it wasn't like the usual seconds dragging by feeling I've had working with him up to now. We talked about what I'd help him with, and it took long enough that I had to write him a note because he was going to be late for P.E.

Everyone knows that Mr. Irons, the gym teacher, can make your life miserable if he wants to, and Kurt even said thanks for the note. When I signed it and said "Ironshorts blows," it was worth the taste of canned beets to get that kid to actually laugh.

Kurt made a quick scan of the park, but after one of the mothers there gave him the stink-eye, he decided he'd better try some other areas for a while. He wandered up one side street and down another, searching for a rescue and the money it'd bring him, but trying hard not to look like he was searching for something.

The air was still and hot as Kurt considered what Will had said earlier that day. He knew his work was bad. He'd missed a lot of school during the last couple of years, and if that Will guy really wanted to help him, then skipping lunch to be tutored was no big deal, really. It wasn't as if anyone would notice whether he showed up in the cafeteria. He ate alone every single day and had since February, when he'd ended up in this loser town. Winter here sucked; it rained or snowed every day, was still dark when he left for school, and was barely still light when he got out at the end of the day. At least his old life in Southern California had had the good weather thing going on, even if everything else about being there had been crap.

Suddenly, a big orange cat stepped out from a driveway across the street. He had the big round head of a tom, and Kurt casually crossed over to get a closer look. The cat had no collar, which was on Carrie's list of owner infractions. The cat's ears were notched with old scars, and Kurt noted that one of his eyes squinted, emitting a line of wet stuff that ran down the side of his nose. *Doesn't look like anyone's taking care of you, does it?* he thought. The cat's ears twitched at a sound or some invisible fly, and then he backed up and sprayed the shrub at the end of the driveway. *You're not fixed, either.* Another broken rule.

Kurt reached into his backpack for the carrier, digging around a bit more for the cellophane-wrapped package of catnip. *Three strikes, cat*—Kurt stepped closer to the marmalade cat—*and you're out.*

Making sure that no one was watching, Kurt held a small wad of catnip in one outstretched hand and held the carrier in the other hand in what he hoped was a nonthreatening manner. The cat shot a look toward him, flattened his ears, and opened his mouth in a tooth-baring hiss before melting into the bushes that lined the driveway.

Whatever, Kurt shrugged. He shoved the catnip in his pocket, disappointed that he hadn't been able to get the cat. Carrie's payoff of forty dollars would have been great. But he worried a little about the cat's eye, which hadn't looked so good. Carrie would have at least done something about that. He continued down the street.

That's what my cat would have looked like, he thought. But his cat was dead. The kitten had only been about six months old when Mark had backed over him with his pickup. He hadn't even been sorry. Just tossed the small striped body onto the lawn and yelled about how this better not make him late for work.

Kurt walked faster, angry that he still had that memory. He was angrier still that he felt tears welling up. He bit hard on the inside of his cheek to erase that feeling. Feeling angry was always better than the helpless feeling of sad. That was definitely a feeling he wasn't ever going to stand again. Just then, a dog barked from a fenced backyard as he passed. *If you're going to have a dog, you should at least pay attention to it.*

Kurt was amazed at how he'd noticed just in the last couple of days how many dogs were shut up in yards, and he began to wonder how hard it would be to get those dogs out. There sure seemed to be a lot of them, and that could mean a lot of cash for him, if he could figure it out.

All of this walking around was making him thirsty. Deciding that the orange cat was a lost cause, at least for today, Kurt headed toward downtown, the thought of a big cold Coke making his feet move even faster.

Carrie sat on the grass between the two headstones. The words *Mother* and *Father* were a comfort to her, and the warm feeling enfolded her like the arms of her parents, both so long gone now. Mavis roamed the tall grass at the edge of the cemetery; Carrie had left the others securely locked up at home. She was losing patience with Penny's never-ending commentary, and Buddy—well, Buddy's whining was getting on her nerves.

She plucked a small white flower from the green of the sloping lawn and twirled it in her fingers. "Mother. Father."

She got no further than this for a moment, thinking of her childhood and how happy she'd been. But Mavis's sharp bark interrupted her thoughts. Carrie turned her head to see the dog flush a pheasant from the brush.

She looked down at the flower in her hand again. "I *have* been taking care of the animals, more of them all the time." Carrie went on to tell her parents about talkative Penny and bouncy Buddy. She left out the part about the two cats, though, especially the poor little black-and-white one.

"There's this boy, Kurt. He's helping me to make up for—what happened before." Carrie looked up and around, searching out Mavis among the gravestones. The big dog bounded across the cemetery, silhouetted against the lowering sun. Satisfied that Mavis was safe, Carrie returned to her conversation.

"All I want is to show you that I can make it all better." Carrie gave her mother's headstone a gentle pat. "And I will." She struggled to her feet, then bent down to give the etched letters spelling out *Father* a pat, too, before calling Mavis. Soon, Carrie steered the sedan out of the cemetery with her usual farewell wave to her family.

The cheeseburger, in all its greasy glory, called to him like a siren from its paper wrapping. Will was ravenous, way too ravenous to wait until he could actually cook something. Why didn't he do this more often? He could eat out every day if he really wanted. The few bucks he dropped here weren't going to make any difference in paying for college or even in meeting the monthly electric or phone bills.

This afternoon, when Claire had mentioned that maybe they could spend their lunch hour together at the track or even just jogging through town, he'd rushed home, laced up his sweat-dampened, smelly running shoes, and forced his legs to run all over again. It felt better today, and the thought of a lunchtime run with Claire tomorrow shoved his physical discomfort to the back of his brain. Any time he could spend with Claire was worth whatever he'd have to go through to make it happen. And if training extra hard was something he had to do to keep from looking stupid or out of breath when he was running with her, then fine.

Lunchtime. Will stopped chewing and scrunched up his face, remembering the plans he'd made to tutor Kurt at lunchtime for the next several days. Irritation hit him, and he bit down hard on the inside of his cheek as he chomped violently on the food in his mouth. "Oww-ch!" A strangled cry of pain escaped him, along with some bits of cheese-burger. Will glanced around and was relieved to find no stares, pointing, or laughter at his plight.

But as he looked up, he saw Claire's cousin Lydia walk by the big windows of the restaurant, pushing the huge new stroller she'd gotten as a gift from her grandparents at the baby shower. Will looked over at the monster stroller. *How much did that thing cost, anyway?* he wondered.

He watched Lydia toss the cigarette from her lips and crush it beneath her platform-soled foot. Leaving the baby outside in the stroller, she entered the fast-food place alone.

The money for that fancy stroller, Will decided, *would have been better spent on parenting classes*. After eyeing the stained tee shirt on the baby, Will watched the back of Lydia's head as she leaned across the counter, chatting with the teenager behind it.

He took another, more careful bite of his burger, careful to chew on the side away from the giant gouge he'd bitten into his cheek. As he worked his way through his burger, he watched out the window as the baby fussed in the stroller. It was getting harder to enjoy his meal, seeing such a little baby out there all alone.

She'll probably sell it for cigarette money, he reflected with a sigh, wondering whether he meant the stroller or the baby.

Although Will didn't consider himself even remotely into babies, as he watched the kid start to cry, he thought about going out there and grabbing him, then delivering him to his oblivious mother. *Anyone could just walk off with that baby, and she wouldn't have a clue*.

But instead of doing anything, Will returned to the remains of his burger. Swallowing the last of it and wiping his mouth with the back of his hand, he saw Kurt approach the front door, then stop and frown at the sight of the now wailing child. Kurt yanked the door open and entered the restaurant.

"Your baby's crying." Kurt's voice carried from the counter to Will. He couldn't make out the girl's reply, but he heard Kurt say, "You better go check. I mean, he's really crying."

Lydia shot an exasperated look at the girl behind the

counter, then stalked out the door, grabbed the handle of the stroller, and cut across the parking lot. Will heard the horn of a car, then watched it pull up to her. One of the boys he'd seen at the party leaned out, and after a few seconds, he handed her a cigarette.

Well, he thought, *she doesn't let a baby interfere with her social life.* Speaking of a social life, he seriously considered telling Kurt that lunchtimes weren't going to work out for tutoring him. The whole big breakthrough this afternoon had been good and all, but if Will had to choose between Kurt and Claire, well, that really wasn't a fair fight. But before Will could come up with a halfway believable excuse to get out of it, Kurt was at his table.

"What should I bring tomorrow?" Kurt asked.

The word *tomorrow* brought on tomato, and Will took a drink of his vanilla shake to wash it away.

Too late, Will thought, the regret almost a physical ache. Then he listed the items and books Kurt would need for their lunchtime session.

"Your baby's crying."

The blonde looked Kurt up and down before leaning back on the counter. "Yeah, well, babies do that." The chick who was supposed to be taking orders giggled.

"You better go check."

The wails made his backbone feel like it was made of ice, and for a second, he felt the memory of the rasp of choked sobs tearing his own throat. The closet had been dark, and it would have been a good hiding place—if only he'd been able to keep quiet. But it didn't take Mark long to find him there and make good on his promise to give him something to really cry about.

Kurt blinked himself back to reality and the fast-food place, and he wished there was some way he could force this girl to go out there and make the sound of that crying go away.

"I mean, he's *really* crying."

The girl threw a look at the counter girl, and Kurt felt a flush of humiliation rise up his neck as the blonde said "kids," obviously including him in that remark, and then left.

Kurt was left staring into the deadpan face of the counter girl. "Can I take your order?" she asked.

His thirst fled as his embarrassment rose. He looked around and noticed Will sitting a few tables away. Relief at seeing a familiar face stopped the reddening of his cheeks. He muttered "No, thanks" to the snotty counter girl and walked over to Will.

"What should I bring tomorrow?"

Will looked up, made a face, and took a drink of his shake before answering.

"Okay," said Kurt, and it did feel okay. *This whole lunchtime thing might work out*, Kurt thought, as he headed back to his grandmother's house. He wasn't happy with his schoolwork and was embarrassed, even. Jeez, in grade school, he'd felt pretty good about being labeled "talented and gifted," but that was before his dad left.

He licked his dry lips, suddenly remembering that he

had wanted a Coke. But there had been no way he was going to give a penny to that snotty chick working at the drive-in. He made a beeline for the mini-mart across the street. *Damn.* The stupid blonde girl was there now, too, her stroller all but blocking the entrance to the store. Kurt weighed his thirst against having to deal with her twice in less than a few minutes.

I bet Grandma's got some Cokes in the fridge.

And then, suddenly remembering it was bingo night and his grandmother wouldn't be home anyway, Kurt shifted his backpack higher on his shoulder and changed direction.

This is beginning to be a regular thing, Carrie thought as she opened her door to find Kurt on the porch once again. He shrugged his shoulders and shook his head in answer to the question in her raised eyebrows. Still without speaking a word, she let him inside. Mavis, Penny, and Buddy fell over each other, tails wagging like flags, interrupting each other in order to get their hellos in.

"Hey, guys," Kurt broke the silence and stooped down low. *To reach them easier*, thought Carrie, but she also suspected it was to keep Mavis's nose out of his crotch.

"It was a warm one today," she remarked, noting the sheen of sweat on the boy's face. Kurt straightened up and ran a sleeve across his forehead, and Carrie again glimpsed the angry red marks on the inside of his arm.

"Would you like something to drink?" When he nodded, she turned and went to the kitchen. "I have milk, lemonade, and iced tea," she called out.

"Do you have any pop?"

Pop? Oh, soda. "Sorry, no." Carrie had never liked that syrupy stuff.

"Then I'll have the lemonade."

She took two tumblers from the cupboard and poured lemonade from the ice-filled pitcher, thinking how lucky it was that she'd just made a new batch. He was still standing by the door when she returned. She pointed one of the tumblers at a chair, saying, "Have a seat."

They sat in silence, sipping their drinks. Carl limped into the room, tail held high. "What do you have there?" he demanded. He gathered himself up and leapt up onto her lap.

"Hello, Carl." Carrie held her glass up and away from the inquisitive cat. "Where's Belle?"

"Still up the tree, I suppose." His gray nose twitched as he stretched his neck toward the glass of lemonade. "She saw your friend here walk up and decided she'd stay out of his way."

Carrie sighed, knowing it was probably true. Cats were funny that way. She lowered the tumbler so it was within his reach and laughed as Carl wrinkled up his nose, then jumped down to head for the kitchen.

"How can you drink that stuff?" the cat asked, before he pushed through the cat door and out into the yard.

"Is he always in a bad mood like that?"

Carrie suddenly remembered she still had a guest. "Who? Carl?"

"Yeah. He always looks like, I don't know, like he ate something that went bad. The cat I tried to get today had that same sort of look."

"Which cat was that?" Carrie put her glass on the coffee table and leaned forward.

"I found this big orange cat on Third Street. Its ears were ripped up pretty bad, and it had this runny eye. I think it was sick or something."

Carrie could see that the boy was concerned, but inwardly, she breathed a sigh of relief. The marmalade cat had made it home in one piece.

"When I tried to get near it, it hissed at me and took off." Kurt looked a little put out at that part of the story.

"I'd give him a couple of days before trying again," Carrie advised. "You just never know what these creatures have gone through. It would be enough, I'm sure, to put *anyone* in a bad mood."

"Like Carl?"

Carrie regarded the boy seated across the coffee table from her. *He's what, fifteen, give or take a year?* He could be her son. She'd never had a child of her own, and now, at 47, she supposed those days were behind her. She'd just never met the right man. None of the boys in school could measure up to her father, and after that, there was the trouble. And she wasn't going to think about *that* tonight.

"Let me tell you *why* Carl has every right to be in any kind of mood he wants," said Carrie.

"Oh, no. Please, Carrie, I hate this story," Mavis whined. Carrie ignored her. Penny and Buddy both looked at her with the same expectancy as Kurt.

"About seven years ago, it was just Mavis and me. We had just come out of a sad spell, losing three of our cats and Tip, our dog, too, all within a few months of each other." The memory of that time still held a sharp edge of grief. "Thank god, I had gotten Mavis from the shelter just before all that." At the sound of her name, Mavis's tail beat against the floor.

"We'd always had a problem with people dumping their cast-off animals on our property. Mind you, it could be puppies, kittens, or even pets that I guess had become too old to bother with."

Carrie stopped and took a drink of her lemonade. *Mother couldn't stand to see a creature suffer or go without. The house was alive with the energy of those animals. Father, bless his heart, never said an unkind word about it.*

"Have you always lived here?" Kurt's eyes held disbelief.

Carrie nodded. "My parents lived here from the day they were married." She took another drink from the sweating glass. "And my father's parents lived here before that. I think they were relieved to hand over the responsibilities of the property and move to a more manageable place in town. I'm the last one left, so . . . It's comfortable, familiar." She forced a smile through the sudden pang of remembering again that they were all long gone. "And it's paid for."

She straightened herself in her chair. "So I wasn't surprised that day to hear a cat crying from the brush along the fence line. I was surprised by what I found, though."

There was a thin gray cat, filthy with dirt and blood, the rope still tied to its rear left leg. One look at that leg, hanging on by nothing more than skin, and the naked, raw patches along the side of its body and head had convinced her that she had precious few minutes to get the poor animal to the vet.

"I found him in the bushes. The veterinarian told me he'd been dragged, probably behind a car. I could have killed whoever did such a horrible thing!" She noticed that Kurt was no longer looking at her, but down at his feet.

"He stayed at the vet's for almost a month, and when no one stepped up to claim him" *or to pay the massive vet bill*, she thought wryly, "he came home with me."

Kurt looked back up at her in the space between her words.

"So I named him Carl, and he's lived here ever since. So that's why I figure he's allowed his bad moods."

The boy remained silent, so Carrie took the plunge. "Pretty bad, huh? That was the worst thing that had ever happened to him, and I make sure it is the worst thing that ever *will* happen to him. So what about you, Kurt? What's the worst thing that ever happened to you?" She held her breath. Had she pushed him too far?

The boy reached his hand over to scratch the inside of his other arm, then stood up quickly, his face unreadable, leaving his half-finished lemonade on the table. "Nothing," he said flatly. "I'd better go. My grandmother's waiting for me."

~

Will looked across the table at Kurt, taking in his sharpened pencil and fresh sheet of blue-lined paper. He shuffled his own papers aside and had Kurt pull up a chair opposite him, then glanced up at the clock to see that they had just under a half an hour to get something accomplished.

"Synonyms and antonyms," Will began. He'd spent his morning run laying out a plan for these extra tutoring sessions and was glad that the kid had actually followed through and showed up prepared. He was also relieved that Claire hadn't seemed mad or anything when he told her that lunchtime runs were out because of tutoring Kurt. And even though he'd done so several times already by now, he replayed the conversation with Claire in his head.

"That's okay," she'd said, when he explained about Kurt. "You're great to do that. I mean, that's a really nice thing to do." Then she smiled at him. Even her teeth were pretty.

Will felt a pleased flush on his neck when she complimented him. "Nice? I don't know. It's kind of for college." And now he wished he'd said something more than that, but then Claire had reached over and laid her hand on his arm. If he'd thought shaking hands with her dad was an electric shock, this was like a thousand lightning storms going through him. For that split second, Claire's hand on his arm was his entire world.

"Well, *I* think it's nice. I think *you're* nice."

"Thanks. You are, too." As soon as the words left his mouth, he looked at her carefully. He wanted to see whether his words sounded as lame to her as they did to him when he said them. But she seemed fine, and then she said she was happy to meet him after school or even on weekends. Weekends with Claire, instead of alone, sounded great to him.

Will was suddenly aware that Kurt was staring at him, and he wondered how long he'd been spacing out. He quickly recovered and continued: "Synonyms are words that—"

"Are the same," Kurt finished.

"Right." Okay, good, at least they didn't have to go back *that* far. "Synonyms are words that have a meaning similar to another word. And antonyms?" Will waited.

"Different," Kurt sighed. He picked up his pencil. "I know this stuff already."

"All right, great. So give me three antonyms for the word"—Will had to stop and remember the words he'd chosen—"*listen* and three synonyms for the word *neglect.*"

The boy immediately bowed his head and began. Will sat back in his chair and watched him write.

"Oh, and you can use your dictionary if you need it," he said. Kurt did not look up from his writing, but scratched a few more marks, then put down his pencil with a snap.

"Here."

Will looked at the scrawled penmanship. Why weren't they doing this on the computers? He squinted and translated the jagged lines into words. Under the word *Listen*, Kurt had written *antonyms* and then below that, *Ignore.* Good. *Disregard*, even better. *Tune-out*, fair enough. Will had felt like he was being tuned-out more times than he could remember.

He moved on to the synonyms under *Neglect*. *Carelessness*, okay. *Inattentivness*. Will wiggled his shoulders at the misspelled word, the taste of vanilla pudding on his tongue clouded by the error, but he was impressed with Kurt's choices. It was way above what Will had expected and quite a contrast to the work that Kurt had turned in so far. Then Will read the last synonym on Kurt's list and was a bit taken aback. *Bad mother*. Those two words somehow seemed to overshadow all the others. It wasn't that the letters were larger or written in a heavier hand. No, they simply stood out.

The fast-food place. Will thought back to the afternoon before and how Kurt had tried to make Claire's cousin go outside and take care of her baby. He'd been glad to see her go and had felt kind of guilty for not being the one to say something. Then he thought back to the time he saw Kurt come in for burgers with his grandmother. Where was his mother? That's when Will realized he knew next to nothing about this kid. His entire opinion of him was based on seeing him lift a cheap lighter and rip down some worthless flyer. That, and the half-done homework he'd turned in. Will looked up to see Kurt watching him and knew he needed to say something.

"Bad mother. That's two words. A true antonym is a single word." He wanted to take his comment back as soon as he spoke. *Will, you dolt!*

Kurt shrugged.

"The rest of them are fine, though," Will added hurriedly.

Kurt shrugged again.

Will changed direction for a moment. "It's an interesting choice—*bad mother*, I mean." Now curious, Will tried again to get him to tell him something. "You just moved here this winter?"

Kurt nodded.

"So where are you and your parents from?"

"My parents are divorced." The statement sounded dead, emotionless.

But Will wasn't ready to give up yet. "So, do you live with your mom or your dad?" He could see the kid start to lose some of that wary look. *Good. See? Won't be long before I make this kid think I'm his new best friend.*

"My grandmother. I'm going to live with my dad, though. He's getting us a place, but he wanted me to finish the school year here."

"And your mom?"

"She doesn't live here." The kid's tone left no room to follow that line of questioning.

Will tried again. "Your grandmother seems nice."

Kurt looked confused.

"I met her at the drive-in."

"Oh, yeah."

"I heard what you said to Lydia there, too. Thanks for doing that."

"Who's Lydia?" The confusion had returned to Kurt's blue eyes.

"She's the blonde girl with the baby. I heard you ask her to go take care of him. I was going to do it myself; I kind of know her, but not really. She's a cousin of, uh, a friend of mine."

"I just told her the kid was crying." Kurt shrugged again. "I don't think she takes care of that baby very well."

"Yeah, you're right about that," Will replied. "I don't know if I'd call her a bad mother, though. Careless, maybe."

Kurt poked his finger at the word *Carelessness* on the paper between them. It was the first synonym he'd listed under *Neglect*. "I don't think she's all that good at it."

Will had to agree. "I guess. Good thing your mom's better than that, right?" And then right away, he tried to correct the mistake. He had meant *grandmother*, not *mom*. But he didn't get the chance.

Kurt stood up quickly, his chair moving backward across the floor with a clatter. He didn't look up as he gathered his papers and books, then shoved them into his backpack. "Yeah. *I guess.*" He looked up, and Will was alarmed to see the look of raw hurt on the kid's face. "Good thing your mom's better than that, right?" And then he was gone.

Will sat for another minute, wishing he could take the last couple of minutes back. At least Claire wasn't around to see the mess he'd made of everything. How nice would she think he was now?

Carrie felt awful about the way she'd run Kurt off the day before. She'd pushed him too hard. She knew it, and she'd have to be a lot more careful with him in the future. *Just like the marmalade cat*, she speculated. *Once spooked, he'll be a lot harder to get close to the next time.*

She sat at her kitchen table, a bowl of untouched soup

steaming before her, the stares of three dogs and two cats directed like lasers at any move she made. "Do you mind?" she complained. The animals didn't budge, and Carrie didn't tell them to go away. She wasn't hungry, anyway. She knew she should be, but when she got upset, she found it impossible to eat a thing. And Kurt's abrupt departure had rattled her.

"You need to eat, Carrie." There was concern in Mavis's voice. But Carrie could also see the raw desire for some of her soup in the big dog's eyes as well as the drool falling from her pink tongue.

"Or not," offered Carl. "Why eat if you're really not hungry? I'd be happy to take that soup off your hands." His gray nose moved as he sniffed the air. "Chicken, is it? I'm here to help."

Carrie stood up from the table, moved the soup bowl to the counter, took four more bowls from the cupboard, and divided the contents into five portions, pouring and re-pouring until she was satisfied they were all equal. Then she put the dishes on the floor, leaving the animals to enjoy the chicken noodle soup, and walked out the back door.

Her feet carried her over the back lawn. *Needs mowing.* She considered calling the service she sometimes used when it got long like this, but with Belle, Penny, and now Buddy here, she decided against it. Too risky. Someone might find out about the animals she and Kurt had rescued. Instead, she'd have to get the mower going on her own. Farther up and over the rise, the little crosses came into view. Carrie walked up and sat near them in the tall grass.

She liked to come here or go to the cemetery when she

was feeling out of sorts like this. How had Carl put it? Gotten herself in a wad again? Yes, that was it. But she felt good, really good, regardless of what Carl thought—or Mavis, for that matter.

The little pills in her medicine chest could just stay where they were. She had no need of them, not now or ever. She'd taken them like a good little girl for way too long. The doctors insisted it was the pills that made her feel better. But she had a nagging feeling that those pills were making her feel dull, half alive, as if she had no purpose in life. That's how it was, too, until she had decided to cut the dose in half.

And then there was that wonderful day, a couple of weeks ago, when Mavis had looked at her and Carrie had *heard* her voice, really heard her. Carl, too. And then Carrie knew absolutely that she'd been right about those pills all along. That day, she had put the pills and those doctors behind her forever.

She lay back in the grass, arms crossed behind her head, watching a contrail progress across the blue ceiling of sky, and thought of shooting stars. She closed her eyes, calming herself, drinking in the peace of the place. *"Make a wish, Carrie."* She could hear her mother's voice. When she took the time to listen, she always heard her mother's voice.

Kurt went directly to his grandmother's after school. Hunting for strays could wait, along with the money they'd bring. First, it had been Carrie asking about parents. And then today, that senior, Will, had acted all concerned about his home life, too.

What am I, some kind of freak show?

He picked up his pace, making the books in his backpack bump almost painfully against the small of his back. He was sick of it here. And now he was sick of all this new attention, too. It hadn't been that bad to finally talk to someone other than his grandmother. But it was bad news when they started sticking their nose into his private family business.

The backpack bumped him even harder, and he reached up to hoist it up off his back.

What was the deal with his dad, anyway? Why hadn't he called? It had been almost four months. No phone calls, no letters, nothing. His grandmother couldn't even tell him the name of the friend he was staying with. Was she keeping him from his dad? She must be. But she'd always been nice to him since he'd come to stay with her. Why would she keep him here when he could be with his dad, where he belonged?

Kurt spotted her in the front yard, watering the small patch of lawn and the line of flowers that separated her property from the next-door neighbor's. He stole a look to make sure that the only car in front was his grandmother's. Then he wished he hadn't. How long was he going to keep checking for that truck he'd never have to see again?

"Hi," she said as he walked up, easing her grip on the spray nozzle to cut the stream. "It's nice to see you home after school for a change. No work today?"

He shook his head. "Later." His grandmother smiled at him in reply and resumed her task.

"Grandma?" When she didn't turn back toward him, he tried again, louder this time. "Grandma!" She jumped and dropped the hose, which skittered away from her feet.

"Kurt, you scared the life out of me. If you really want to talk to me, please turn off the water."

Kurt turned the tap, heard the high-pitched note of the water pressure fade, and then turned to her. "I want to talk to my dad. I want his telephone number now."

His grandmother's mouth moved silently for a couple of seconds before any words came out. "Give it a little more time."

"Please, I know you have a number for him."

She sighed and wiped her wet hands on the sides of her slacks. "Okay, Kurt. Come inside."

They entered the house together. The curtains were open and the television wasn't on, and those two factors made the living room seem like it belonged to someone else. "Aak! The furniture will fade in no time in this light." She moved to shut the drapes against the glare of the late spring sun.

"No, Grandma. It looks better this way. I can actually *see*, for once." Her hand stopped short of the heavy drapes. "My dad's number?" he reminded her.

"He's going to call you soon, Kurt. Why don't you stop your worrying for now and let him get settled?" She lit a cigarette, but Kurt saw her hand tremble as she held the lighter.

"I'm not waiting anymore." His tone made clear his frustration.

Her shoulders slumped forward as she picked her purse up and pulled a slip of paper from her wallet. Kurt took it, reading the numbers. It was only white paper and blue ink, but it was the closest he'd been to his dad in months. He moved toward the phone, his heart in his throat.

"Wait," she said.

He stopped, exasperated by her interference. He was tired of all the reasons she came up with not to call his dad. He was going to call him today, right now, no matter what she said.

"I was hoping he'd tell you himself." She took a long drag off her cigarette, leaving him standing there, waiting. "But your dad's been getting a new life together, with his new job and a place to live. And he's been moving on with other things, too."

"Like what?" Kurt couldn't imagine where she was going with all this. "What are you talking about?"

"He met someone, honey."

"So?"

"He's *married*, Kurt. Your dad got *married*."

The friend? The friend he was supposed to be sharing a place with to save money? That friend was supposed to be some guy, not a woman, and especially not a wife.

Now his ears roared, and the floor seemed to tilt. He felt like he'd somehow stepped into a parallel universe. It was the same place, but *not* the same.

"When?" was all he managed to say.

"It's been a couple of months now."

"I have to go to work." The slip of paper floated from Kurt's fingers as he grabbed his backpack and walked past his grandmother out the front door.

He was almost at the end of the block before he remembered to breathe again. He leaned against a telephone pole to gasp for air and keep his legs from buckling. His father had been married for two months—two whole months—and no one had told him. Not his grandmother, and obviously not his dad. Even his mom, with all of her "I'm taking responsibility" crap, hadn't said anything about it in her letter.

I guess that *isn't one of the things she thinks she's responsible for.*

As he leaned, something crinkled beneath his shoulder blades, and he turned around to look. It was a poster for Belle, only this time the reward was a hundred dollars. Why would they spend money to find something they didn't take care of in the first place? Kurt had no idea. But he'd be happy to make sure they never had another chance to let Belle wander where something bad could happen to her.

He returned to Third Street, where he'd seen the big orange cat, and started poking around in the bushes where it had disappeared. He wanted that cat and the forty bucks it would bring him. Just a few more animals, and he'd have enough for a bus ticket to get as far away as he wanted.

It was obvious to him now why his dad hadn't called him. A new wife? A new *life* is more like it. She probably had kids, too—perfect kids. His dad could start all over, with perfect kids this time, and not have to worry about him anymore. Had he *ever* worried about him? Kurt used to wonder about it when he was younger, when he still saw his father a couple of times a month. But that was before Mark got really bad. And whenever Kurt would ask to go live with his dad, he would say that Kurt was better off with his mom, who'd do a better job. By the time his mom got worse and Mark didn't think twice about knocking him around, his dad had moved away. By then, Kurt was lucky if he even got to talk to him once a month. No, you definitely don't worry about someone you talk to only once a month. And now, not calling him for four months? What's an antonym for *worry*?

He didn't want to live in Minneapolis with his dad anyway, he decided. *Too cold.* He started thinking of other places where he could go. Someplace that was warm all year, for sure. And someplace where he could find a job and get his own place, too.

Just then, a sharp yip and a whine caught his attention, and he looked past the driveway and the house—right into the face of a dog. A dog of enormous size stood on its hind legs, with its head and front paws showing over the top of a fence that was almost as tall as Kurt. The dog yipped again, its mouth open in a panting grin. The grin was infectious, and Kurt felt his anger begin to fade.

"Hey, there." He looked around, then over his shoulder to make sure he wasn't being watched. He approached the huge animal slowly, talking to it under his breath. "What's going on, huh?" The dog dropped down to all fours, and Kurt raised himself cautiously on his toes to peer over the wooden slats into the yard. The dog was watching for him, its long tail whipping back and forth, slapping against its sleek flanks.

"Oh, god," he said under his breath, as he took in the patchwork of holes and dead grass and the piles of dog poop everywhere. Despite the hot day, there was no shade for the dog. And one look at the dust-coated plastic dish showed that there hadn't been water in it for a while, either.

He reached over the gate and raised the latch, careful not to make a sound as he swung it open. Nobody appeared to be home, and there didn't seem to be any sign of human activity anywhere. Kurt slid sideways through the opening in the gate and held out his hand to the dog. The sound of a radio suddenly blared from the open window above his head. Kurt stood still, willing himself to become invisible. Over the pounding in his chest, he heard a man's voice singing along, loud and off-key.

Mark's voice? No. Not *Mark's voice*.

The adrenaline rushed through him, even as he inwardly yelled at himself to stop freaking out, that it was just some guy, some guy who didn't even know he was in his yard. It took every bit of his will not to bolt. Kurt slowed his breathing and forced his feet to walk back to the gate. He slipped through the opening. The gate closed behind him with a soft click, and Kurt quickly left the dog and the singing man. There were easier ways than this to get his forty bucks.

He made the park his next stop, sitting down heavily on the bench. The park was quiet. No kids screamed from the playground this afternoon, and he closed his eyes to catch his breath. The day wasn't even over yet, but to Kurt it felt like three or four days combined. He was exhausted.

"Excuse me."

Kurt looked up, startled. A woman offered him a sheet of paper from a stack under her arm. He recognized her immediately. She was Buddy's owner.

"Have you seen this dog?" The black curly-haired dog stared at him from the photocopy.

The feeling he'd had toward her the other day, when Buddy had almost been hit by the car, returned a hundred-fold. Carrie had said losing her dog would be a good lesson for this woman, and he now agreed wholeheartedly. *Take care of your animals, or you won't have them anymore.* He almost shook with anger. His arm itched like mad, and he fought the urge to scratch it.

"Nope" was all he managed to croak.

"Would you mind taking this?" she continued, her forehead lined with deep ridges.

Kurt took the sheet without a word. He got up from the bench, dropping the flyer in the trash on his way out of the park. He walked and pondered until the day fell into twilight, when his stomach told him it was past dinnertime. He headed downtown to the fast-food restaurant.

By the time Kurt finished his second cheeseburger, it was dark, and he thought about going home.

Home? What home?

So instead, he walked again, sticking to the side streets of town, taking in the glows coming through the squares of windows. He thought about heading out to Carrie's. It would feel good to see Buddy and just hang out with Mavis. But after last night, he was worried that Carrie would ask him if there was something wrong, and he really wasn't up to answering that question. He smirked a little at that thought. For the past few years, there'd always been something wrong. But had *anyone* ever asked him *anything* about it? Not his *dad*, that's for sure.

He rounded a corner and squinted against the glare of headlights as a car slowed and then stopped.

"Kurt!" Carrie's voice floated through the rolled-down window, and Kurt saw Mavis resting her chin on the back of the passenger seat. "Do you need a ride?"

Why not? He walked over to the car and got in.

Mavis pushed her head over the seat and nuzzled his neck. Kurt grimaced at the tickle and twisted around to pet her brown and black fur.

"Out looking for animals? That's what we're doing, too. Haven't had any luck yet. Doesn't look like you have, either. The night's still young, though."

Kurt had a hard time following what she was saying. He'd never heard her talk this much all at once—or so fast, either. But she also sounded happier than he'd ever heard her. And not just regular happy, but super happy. It'd been a long time since he had been around anyone having this good of a time. Mavis gave him another nudge with her long nose, and he let himself smile.

"So what do you think? Do you want to look together? Usually, it's just Mavis and me, but it might be good to have someone else to talk to, for a change. Besides, I've already heard all her jokes."

"Sure." Carrie was acting a little weird, but it was better than walking around all by himself in the dark. Maybe he'd get lucky and make some money tonight, after all. It might even be kind of fun.

He watched her shift into Drive, and they started off down the street. She didn't mention his seat belt, so Kurt didn't bother to put it on. It made him feel free. That, and

the novelty of just cruising around in the night with someone in such a good mood, made him feel like for once,
maybe anything was possible and that he could do just
about anything he wanted. Right now, what he wanted most
was not to worry about his mom, his dad, school, or anything else.

Carrie continued her chatter, punctuating it with silly
jokes, riddles, and remarks to Mavis that sounded so much
like one-sided cell phone conversations that Kurt almost
laughed out loud. Suddenly, she stopped the car and her
comedy routine.

"Shhh!" Kurt's eyes followed in the direction she was
pointing. A cat sat in the pool of light under a streetlamp.
It didn't seem particularly concerned about them and just
sat there, blinking in their general direction.

"Do you want to go?" Carrie's eyes twinkled, and in
the dim light of the car, her happy face looked almost like
a kid's. Kurt looked at the cat again and nodded, feeling a
half smile on his face, too. He dug around in his backpack,
past the homework and the books, until he felt the vinyl of
the collapsible pet carrier. He took it out and carefully
stepped out of the car.

The cat stood up, tail raised at his approach. Kurt bent
down low and held his hand out toward the light gray tabby.
But the cat merely shifted its weight from side to side and
pirouetted in a small circle on the sidewalk. Kurt began unzipping the carrier, but at the first rip of sound, the cat
skipped sideways and took off into the bushes next to the
darkened house.

"He'll be fine, Mavis." He heard Carrie's voice from

the car and looked back toward it. He saw her making shooing motions at the bushes where the cat had disappeared and heard her say, "In there! The cat's in there!"

Kurt finished unzipping the bag, then slowly, quietly made his way to the thick clump of bushes. He had to get all the way down on his stomach to see under them.

"Here, kitty," he called, his voice no louder than a whisper. "Come 'ere, kitty." Two points of light—eyes—suddenly appeared through the dark of the leaves, only about a foot and a half from his face. An easy reach and catch, if he could just grab the cat by the scruff of its neck. He inched his hand forward, and the beady eyes blinked. *Man, does this cat have freaky-looking eyes!*

He'd moved his hand only another couple of inches when the bushes seemed to explode. Kurt, still on his belly, scuttled back faster than he thought possible. It felt like the best thing to do, considering the open jaws and pointy teeth of the hissing possum running rapidly toward him.

"Aaiee!" he shrieked as he leapt up and stumbled backward. The pissed-off possum was motivation enough for Kurt to sprint across the yard and jump back into the car before the thing got any closer.

"Did you see that—?" he began, his heart pounding so fast that it was hard to breathe and talk at the same time. He looked over at Carrie and saw that her head was down, her shoulders shaking. *Wait. Is she crying?* "No," he began again, suddenly worried that something was wrong. "It's okay, Carrie. It didn't bite me or anything."

As she raised her head up, Kurt saw that yes, she did have tears running down her cheeks. But she wasn't crying; she was laughing.

"Kurt!" Her words came out in short bursts between her now loud gales of laughter. "Kurt, you should have seen the look on your face!" More laughter then, and she pounded the steering wheel with both fists.

"Hey," Kurt protested, his feelings a little hurt at being made fun of. But the more Carrie howled, the harder it was for him not to join in, and soon both of them filled the car with laughter. Every time they subsided, Carrie let out a muffled snort, sending them both into uncontrolled roars once again. Mavis whined and tried to climb over the seat into the front, but Kurt gently pushed her back.

"Okay," Carrie said, finally pulling the car out from the curb. "I'm thirsty now." She looked over at Kurt, and he rubbed his damp eyes with the back of his sleeve. "You must be, too. Want a soda? I mean a pop?"

Kurt nodded, unsure whether he could speak without cracking up all over again.

"Shall we go to the fast-food restaurant? I haven't been there in years."

Kurt glanced at the small clock in the car. It said 10:37. Could that be right? How long had he been walking around before Carrie picked him up? "It's gotta be closed by now."

"So I'll buy you something to drink at the mini-mart," she said, making a right at the next stop sign.

This is what feeling good really feels like, Carrie thought as she moved the scythe through the tall grass surrounding the grave markers. With each swipe, she felt the currents of energy run through her arms and wondered why she'd left the old tool unused for so long in the shed. This was so much better than that loud, smoky mower. The cut grass flew in a swinging rhythm into the sunset sky, a lovelier sky than she had ever seen. It was so beautiful, it almost hurt to look at it.

The job finished now, she lay the blade down and wiped her hands on her slacks. Feeling the catch of her skin on the fabric, she stared at the broken blisters lining the tops of her palms. She'd never even felt a thing.

"Mavis!" she called. Mavis raised her head from where she was sleeping beside the back steps. "Mavis! Come here!" She was excited now. This was a good sign, a happy sign. Mavis arrived at her side, tongue lolling out after bounding up the hill. "See, Mavis!" Carrie showed the big dog her blisters. Mavis sniffed at them carefully, then licked one palm.

"Does it hurt?" Mavis's eyebrows were raised in concern.

Carrie bent down and lifted Mavis's front paws until she was up on her hind legs, now almost as tall as Carrie. She danced the dog around in a circle on the cut grass. "It doesn't hurt at all!" She laughed, delighted. "It's the last part, the last part!"

"Last part?" Mavis panted.

Carrie dropped the dog's paws, and Mavis landed with a soft "oof." Her happiness marred by the question, Carrie struggled to regain her elation and was overjoyed to find it sitting right there in the front of her brain, as beautiful as the sunset.

"The last part I need to make it all better." She scowled down at the dog. Why didn't she understand? "First"—Carrie tried to slow down a little, so Mavis might understand better—"I didn't need to sleep anymore." She nodded at Mavis, hoping for some sense of recognition. Finding none, she continued. "And then, hello? Food?" She threw up her hands to the fading sky. "Don't need it. Not anymore, not ever."

"Food?" asked Mavis, her face a map of hope.

"No!" Carrie snapped, but her huge smile returned immediately, and she reached down to reassure the cowed dog. "No food." She dropped to her knees to embrace Mavis in her happiness. "And now, no pain, either, Mavis. Isn't it wonderful?"

"You're happy, Carrie?" Mavis cocked her head.

"I'll be even happier when we go for a ride later," Carrie answered. "I have a good feeling about what we'll find after dark."

"We're going for a ride?" The hopeful look was back on the big dog's face.

"You know it!" Carrie gave her one last pat, and together, they walked back to the house.

Carrie had always known that she was a pretty good judge of what was what, and when her headlights illuminated the figure on the darkened sidewalk and she saw that it was Kurt, she knew that tonight was no exception. She had been right to tell Mavis earlier that good things would happen this evening. Seeing Kurt definitely qualified as a good thing. "What did I tell you, Mavis?" Carrie smiled. "I told you we'd be happy with what we'd find after dark."

Kurt was quiet when he got into the car, but Carrie didn't mind. The night was warm; the smell of that sweet spring air and new flowers made it feel like anything was possible. The boy must feel that way, too. Carrie could see how well he and Mavis got on, and he didn't seem to mind that Carrie was doing most of the talking.

Oh sure, Mavis got her two cents in. She was actually rather amusing tonight, and as the lively banter with the dog escalated, Carrie stole a look at Kurt. He was smiling, looking like there might be a laugh inside him somewhere.

She sucked in a quick gulp of air. Could he be hearing Mavis, too? Carrie was certain that if he didn't hear the dog now, he soon would. She returned her attention to the street ahead of her. Another surge of happiness swept her up. Kurt was ready to really listen. She was sure of it.

She suddenly stomped on the brake as a cat caught her eye, sitting in a pool of light from a streetlamp. "Shhh!" she said, pointing to it. She saw Kurt turn to look. "Do you want to go?" she asked, feeling silly as a schoolgirl. Kurt got out of the car, and Carrie watched as he stealthily approached the cat.

Suddenly, she felt a cold nose on the back of her neck. "He'll be fine, Mavis." But as Carrie was speaking she saw the cat spook and run to the hedgerow at the side of the house. Kurt stood and looked back at her. "In there!" Carrie gestured toward the shrubbery. "The cat's in there!"

Away from the glow of the streetlamp, the yard was dark. Carrie could just make out Kurt's form as he lowered himself, snakelike, onto the grass and started poking around. His frantic scramble backward startled her at first.

But at the sight of the furiously hissing possum and Kurt's pop-eyed shock, she burst into laughter. By the time Kurt scurried back to the car, Carrie was laughing so hard, the only thing she could do was lower her head, her shoulders shaking in silent spasms, and wait for her breath to return so that she could speak.

"Kurt!" Her words finally came out now, between her gales of laughter. "Kurt, you should have seen the look on your face!" Another wave overcame her, and she pounded the steering wheel with both fists. Tears were streaming down her cheeks.

It started off slowly, but soon Kurt, too, was roaring with laughter. She'd never heard him laugh before, and she couldn't remember the last time she'd laughed like this herself. Carrie's stomach ached from it, and her face felt stretched and sore, too. She felt *fantastic*.

"Okay," Carrie said, finally moving her sedan away from the curb. "I'm thirsty now." She looked over at Kurt and watched him rub his damp eyes with the back of his sleeve. "You must be, too. Want a soda? I mean, a pop?" She wanted to do something for him, something to keep him as happy as he seemed right now.

He nodded.

"Shall we go to the fast-food restaurant? I haven't been there in years."

Carrie searched her brain, trying to recall the last time she'd eaten there. Why, they had still had car service then. It was always such a treat to go there with her parents for a quick bite of burgers and malteds on warm summer evenings. She could still see the high school girls in their red-and-yellow uniforms and their white paper hats, delivering the trays piled high with food that would hang on the outside of their car window. She'd secretly wanted to be one of them, but she was such a nervous girl, she knew it was out of the question.

"It's gotta be closed by now," Kurt reminded her.

A stab of regret dampened her mood for a moment. It would've been nice to relive one of those lovely nights. But then she remembered all the remodeling the restaurant had been through over the years. It wouldn't have been the same, anyway. "So I'll buy you something to drink at the mini-mart," she decided, and made a right at the next stop sign. The main street was quiet, and Carrie began to pull into the convenience store's empty parking lot.

"Oh, no." Kurt's moan made her stop in mid-turn and put her foot on the brake.

"What's wrong?" asked Mavis from the back seat, her head between theirs.

"What's wrong?" Carrie echoed. It had been going so well.

"It's that girl and her baby again." He tipped his chin toward the side of the building, and Carrie saw the large stroller parked there. She looked back at Kurt and saw his distress.

"She doesn't take care of that baby, and it cries all the time. She smokes around it with her stupid friends, and I just don't want to deal with any of this tonight."

"It?" Carrie was confused. "You're talking about a *baby*?" She turned to look at the stroller again. "A baby isn't an *it*."

"I know." Kurt's voice sounded upset. "But I don't know if it's a boy or a girl. I only know I can't watch her treat the kid like that anymore."

"Carrie?" Mavis whined and paced in the back seat. "Is there a baby in that stroller? All by itself?" Mavis whined louder. "That's not good. That's not good."

"Quiet, Mavis." Carrie reached back to give the dog a pat. "Is that right, Kurt? There's a baby in the stroller, all by itself, in a parking lot, at"—she looked at the clock— "almost eleven o'clock at night?"

He nodded, and Carrie could still see his discomfort. "I'd better leave," Kurt said, and he started to reach for the door.

No. This was not what she wanted. They'd all been feeling so good and happy, and everything had been so perfect until Kurt saw that stroller. And now he wanted to leave. Her brain raced through her options, but before she could come up with anything, he was already out the door.

"Thanks for the ride," he said. Then he grabbed his backpack and was off down the street.

Carrie looked down at the empty seat next to her. It wasn't quite empty; Kurt had forgotten to fold the pet carrier and put it into his backpack. She backed up and parked on the street instead of in the lot, then killed the lights, but not the engine. She picked up the carrier and left the car to approach the store, leaving the car door ajar and ordering Mavis to stay put.

The energy she had felt earlier in the day had returned full force, and it was humming through her with every step. She peeked into the stroller. The baby slept, shaded from the bug-swarmed streetlamp by the cinder-block wall of the building. She furtively looked around the corner and saw a young blonde girl thumbing through a magazine. That must be the "she" that Kurt had meant.

What in the world is wrong with that girl?

Retreating back into the shadows, Carrie assessed the situation. There were no cars in the lot in front of the store and no kids congregating under the graffiti-covered pay phone. Traffic on the street was nonexistent. And the girl still had not looked up from her magazine, not during the entire time Carrie had been watching her.

Carrie opened the vinyl bag wide. It only took a few seconds, and then they were back in the car. A minute later, she caught up with Kurt, who hadn't gotten far.

"I have something to show you," she said, her voice a happy singsong as she pulled over.

"I have to get home. . . ." Kurt began. He didn't slow his steps, and Carrie kept the car moving in order to stay next to him. "It's late," he continued.

"Come on," she said. "This is good." She smiled, excited at the surprise she had in store for him. "It's *really* good. We just need to get him back to the house, and then I'll bring you right home, I promise."

Mavis barked from the back seat. "Show him, Carrie! Let him see what's in the carrier."

"Mavis wants you to come, too. Can't you hear her?" She saw his signature shrug and stopped the car to let him in. She drove off down the street, but not too fast. No need to attract attention. It wasn't but another minute or two until they were heading out of town.

"So what did you want to show me?" Kurt finally asked. He sounded tired, but Carrie knew he'd perk up right away.

"Here," she said, as she carefully lifted the pet carrier up off the seat and put it on his lap.

"Did you get that cat?" he asked. The vinyl bag moved on his lap. "Wow, this is a really heavy cat." Kurt looked over at her, a look of suspicion spreading across his face.

Carrie smiled back, hardly able to contain her excitement.

"Wait a minute," he said, starting to shove the bag back toward her. "This isn't that possum, is it? There better not be a possum in here!"

"No!" she laughed, and Mavis joined her. "Just look!"

"Is he looking, Carrie?" Mavis was so excited that she hoisted herself halfway over the seat to shove her nose at the bag.

A small whimper came through the mesh of the carrier. Kurt lifted it up and peered through the holes. Carrie saw Kurt's eyes widen almost as huge as when the possum came at him.

Carrie felt like that mischievous schoolgirl again as soon as Kurt knew what he was holding. Nope. It wasn't the possum at all.

Will's Blog: I haven't been talking to myself so much. It's weird, almost as if I realized I forgot to take showers or breathe.

It's been really good, hanging with Claire, running with her, and talking to her. I talk about only good stuff with her, and none of the other things. She hasn't asked me about my brother or what happened to my mom, and there's no way I'm ever going to bring *that* up, either. Being with her almost makes me feel like I can be a different person and that my life and even my past can be anything I want them to be. I know it's not true, and she's probably just being nice by not asking questions, but it's way better than having her feel sorry for me. Who wants to hang out with someone they pity?

I think I actually might be done feeling sorry for myself, too. I mean, the world is full of orphans, isn't it? I can't be the only person who's had bad things happen to them.

Orphan—now, that's an interesting-tasting word. I've eaten something that tastes like it only once. My mom found the recipe in some magazine article about holiday parties. I don't know what she was doing, reading an article like that. She wasn't exactly the party-giving type. But she made one of the recipes in that article that year. She called it *flan*, but it tasted like pudding—the best pudding I've ever had. I wanted her to make it again, but after my dad left, she pretty much stopped cooking. So it was back to the supermarket vanilla pudding in the disposable cups. The word *pudding* is all about the word *inattentive* to me. And when I think about it, pudding in disposable containers really is a perfect match for the word *inattentive*. How attentive can you be to something you're just going to end up throwing away? But it wasn't until they told me my mother was dead—when I overheard a nurse say "or-phan"—that I really noticed the taste connection to flan.

I've been thinking about Kurt, too, and what he wrote about the bad mother. It didn't really seem like he was talking about Lydia. He didn't even know her name. And he sure doesn't know that baby. But he cared enough about it to confront her. That's more than I did. I should have been the one who stood up to her. But when have I ever stood up to anyone?

Maybe he was talking about his own mom. That would make more sense. I feel so stupid about the remark I made about her. I didn't mean to bring up his mom—I meant his grandmother. Maybe I said *mom* because his grandmother looked kind of like my mom. I don't know.

Would he think my mom was bad if he knew what she was like? I never really thought of her that way. I mean, she never did anything to me, like hit me or anything. But she pretty much never did anything, period. Neglectful? I guess. She had other things to think about—I knew that. Maybe she wanted to think about her trips to the doctor and her medicines or my brother's crash and burn more than she wanted to think about being a good mother. Maybe that kind of drama was more interesting to her. She wasn't the best listener, that's for sure.

But I don't want to talk about any of that anymore, even to myself. I'd rather talk about having a girl actually wanting to hang with me, one who thinks I'm okay instead of two steps from crazy. One who doesn't think I'm a whiner. That's what I want.

Whoa. The kids next door just shot off a bottle rocket.

It exploded right outside my window. Stupid kids. But the sparkles looked kind of cool, almost like a shooting star. Can you make a wish on a bottle rocket?

Anyway, if anyone is reading this, I might not be posting much for a while—or maybe ever again. Like I said, talking to Claire is much better than talking to myself, so that's what I'm going to try and do from now on. I guess I'll say *later*. At least, that's what I mean, but since it tastes so much better, I'll say *good-bye* instead.

PART 2

"Carrie . . . " Kurt's voice was a higher pitch than usual; he sounded even more upset than he had when he'd pointed out the stroller at the market, and it grated on her nerves. "We can't keep it! It's a baby, not a cat or dog. We gotta go back. We gotta go back now." Carrie could barely make out Kurt's words through his deep intakes of air.

The dogs surrounded them, noses pushed forward and sniffing furiously as soon as they entered the house, the smaller dogs' questions jumbled with their confusion. At least Mavis was keeping out of it, and Carl, too. He just sat looking at the scene with his usual sour expression. That was fine. As long as he kept his thoughts to himself right now, it was just fine with Carrie.

"What would you have had me do?" Carrie thrust the child into Kurt's arms so she could shut the front door. The last thing she needed was for the little ones to get loose. "Just leave him there?"

Kurt stared at her, horrified. The baby shifted in his arms, and he looked down at him as if he'd just dropped from the sky. Kurt held the baby out to Carrie, and she took him.

116

"'She doesn't take care of that baby.' That's what you told me, correct?" Kurt nodded mutely, seemingly unaware of Buddy madly scratching his pant leg for attention. "You said that it cries all the time; that she and her friends actually smoke around such a little baby." Carrie fixed him with a stern look. She needed Kurt to focus. "You were absolutely right. She doesn't take care of him." Kurt didn't reply. Why was he suddenly being so difficult? "That was all pretty clear when I saw this little one left outside, all alone in the dark, where anyone could have walked off with him. . . ." She stopped and took a breath, beginning to feel upset, too. "*A baby*. Left in a *parking lot*. For the life of me, I'll never understand some people."

"Carrie," Kurt began again. With that, she reached out and grabbed his arm, pushing the sleeve of his shirt up and exposing his scars. He froze, his already pale face even whiter now. For a moment, he didn't even seem to see her.

"Kurt!" she said sharply. The baby startled and then relaxed again. She was glad that Kurt seemed to snap back. She let go of his arm and smoothed the sleeve back down, but he was still silent. "Kurt," she said in a softer voice. "You told me the mother smokes. That her bad friends do, too." She looked intently into his face and then brought the baby closer to him. She watched his posture stiffen.

How could he be afraid of such a little baby?

She ran a finger across the soft yellow hair and then down the inside of one pink arm. "Do you really want," she asked, measuring her words carefully, "to see this tiny arm with the same marks you have on it?"

"No. Oh, God, no." His voice was a plea, and that made

her happy again. "Good. Now that that's settled, let's see what we have here." Carrie held the baby away from her for a moment, scrutinizing. *This one certainly hasn't been missing many meals*, she thought, noting the fat cheeks and the creases at the wrists and elbows. It was a grubby thing though, with stains caking the bunnies on the tiny tee shirt, and a nose that needed wiping. She sniffed. *A diaper change, too*. She was pretty sure now that the rumblings coming from the baby were from a little more than just gas.

"That's poop." Penny's voice came from down at her feet. "I've seen these things before. They poop a lot."

"Great," muttered Carl, flicking his tail. "I'm leaving."

Carrie pulled the baby's soggy diaper forward a bit, peered in, and saw that she was holding a boy and that Penny was correct about the contents of his plastic pants. "You're right, this little *fellow* does need a change."

She looked up to see Kurt staring at her, fear playing over his face. "Listen, it's okay," she said. And to her, it was. It was more okay, she decided, than since her parents had still been here, since the time when they were still a real family.

Kurt walked home from Carrie's house, since there was no way she could leave the baby alone to give him a lift. And there was no way he was riding back to town in that car with the baby in it. By staying away from that baby, maybe he could pretend that this part of the night had never happened.

He'd nearly lost it back at Carrie's, especially when she grabbed his arm. Nobody'd grabbed him like that since that last time, when Mark wouldn't let him go. No matter how hard Kurt had struggled, Mark's grip was too strong. Tonight, that same panic had returned just at the mere memory of what had happened.

He punched himself on the thigh to force that feeling to go. The blow made the two twenties crinkle in his pocket. He had been taken aback when Carrie handed him the cash, but she insisted. "A deal's a deal. You're the one who found him." Then she gave him back the vinyl carrier, saying, "And don't forget to check on that orange tabby."

The baby might be better off with Carrie, he told himself. Maybe. Right? She seemed pretty sure that this was for the best, and at least she didn't smoke. Wasn't that better? Wasn't it?

His mom had smoked, and she hadn't taken good care of him. But his grandmother smoked, too. Did that make her a bad grandmother? No. He wasn't going to believe that. Maybe it wasn't really her fault that his dad had gotten married and not told him. Maybe she was just trying to be a good mother to his dad, giving him a chance to tell Kurt about it himself. Was that why she didn't say anything?

Kurt wanted to ask her about it, but he was sure she'd be asleep when he got back. The crowbar would get him in, no matter how late it was. The thought of the crowbar made him stop in his tracks. His grandmother locked the house every night, whether he was home or not, and she knew he didn't have a key. She'd meant to get him one when he first arrived, but then Kurt had taken off his window lock and didn't need it after all, so he never brought it up. How long had his grandmother known about that? He made up his mind to ask her about *that* in the morning, too.

He continued on toward the glow of the main drag. Then the extra lights, red and blue, spinning over the street and the walls of the mini-mart, revved his pulse again. He counted four cop cars in the lot. Two were sheriffs, and the other two were state troopers. A row of spectators stood at the line of yellow tape surrounding the convenience store, but Kurt didn't join them. He didn't want anyone asking questions about why he was still out at this hour. He forced himself to maintain a casual pace until he rounded the corner, and then, unable to slow his feet any longer, he ran like hell. Soon, Kurt slipped through his window, grateful for the protective comfort of his room.

Will had plans to meet up with Claire later in the afternoon, but he decided to go out for a short run this morning, anyway. Even though it was Saturday, he had awakened without the alarm clock and found himself actually wanting to get out there and run. Sunlight fell across his back from his kitchen window as he bent to tie his shoes. *Gonna be a good day*, he thought, surprising himself with this unaccustomed optimism.

He started off slowly down the street, warming up his muscles and feeling no need to push it. After 20 minutes of winding down side streets, Will headed home. The sun felt warmer now, and either that or the endorphins flooding his bloodstream put him in an even better mood. The blocks passed almost effortlessly. As he got close to his house, he slowed at the sight of his next-door neighbor, who waved him over.

"Hey," Will panted.

The woman looked up from the newspaper she held, her face serious. "Have you seen this?" she asked. Will looked down at the screaming headline and the photo that filled the front page: it was Lydia's baby.

The baby lay sleeping in Carrie's arms, wrapped in one of her father's old undershirts. The fabric was soft against her skin, and she knew the baby must be enjoying the same comfort. She used up the last of the milk in her refrigerator. At first, the infant had had trouble drinking from the teacup Carrie held to his lips. But after several attempts, he had managed to drink, and now the little boy nodded off.

The dogs were understandably concerned at the small bundle of strange smells. Carl couldn't have cared less, and Belle . . . Carrie wondered when the calico would truly join the family. She was still so distant.

Carrie traced her fingertip around the baby's soft, slack mouth. She couldn't keep calling him "the baby," and she wondered what his name was. Not that it mattered, really. That name belonged in his past now. Carrie shifted his weight and looked at her father's undershirt again, trying to remember exactly what had driven her to look for it in the attic. She had plenty of her own shirts that would have worked just fine.

Then her eyes widened at a thought. Could it be? She could hardly bring herself to hope. For all these solitary years, she'd talked to her parents, always searching for signs that they heard her and were saying, yes, she was doing the right thing. Going after the shirt had been a message—her father was helping her. Tears sprang into her eyes. She had missed that help so much after he died.

Carrie snuggled the slumbering baby close to her, taking in the combined aromas of the sleeping infant and the older, more familiar smell of her father. His headstone read "Theodore Williams," although she'd never heard anyone call him that. He'd always answered to Teddy. She searched the features on the little face and saw that it must be true. "Oh, Teddy," she breathed. Carrie smiled lovingly down at him and rejoiced as Teddy opened his eyes and smiled back.

It took a long time before Kurt finally relaxed into sleep. Later, he felt more like a deep-sea diver resurfacing than someone waking up. His eyes felt crusty, and he rubbed them, feeling grit on his cheeks and forehead. He remembered his mad dash the night before and thought it'd be a good idea to wash off the salt of old sweat.

He came into the kitchen a few minutes later, still toweling off his wet hair. His grandmother was at the kitchen table, newspaper open in front of her. Kurt moved the ashtray with the smoldering remains of a cigarette and sat down beside her. "Grandma?" he began, ready to ask her all the things he wanted to know.

"I just can't believe this," she said, fumbling for a new cigarette before Kurt steered the one that was already lit toward her. "I've lived in this town for over 40 years. Your father was *born* here. And in all that time, nothing like this has ever happened."

Kurt looked over her shoulder as she snapped the newspaper to reveal the front page. The face of the baby Carrie had snatched stared back at him. The kitchen seemed suddenly full of twirling red and blue lights, and sweat trickled down his neck.

"Honey," his grandmother asked, "are you feeling all right?"

He knew his face must be pale. The tutoring session with Will came back to haunt him. *Pale:* wan, ashen, drained of color. He could not, however, come up with a synonym to fit what he was feeling inside. *Terrified* didn't even scratch the surface. "I ate at the fast-food place," he answered her. "Maybe I got a bad cheeseburger."

"Can I get something for you?"

His conscience tweaked at her look of concern. "I'm okay." Kurt wanted to take at least that small worry from her shoulders.

She gave him a relieved smile, returning to the paper. "I hope they catch this guy," she said. His grandmother shook her head as she stamped out her cigarette. "The world is full of crazies."

"Yep," he answered, trying to keep his voice from trembling. "Maybe I'll lie down for a while."

She reached out and patted his hand. "That's a good idea. I'll look in on you later."

Kurt left his grandmother at the table to return to his room, realizing as he closed the door that he had forgotten to ask her all those questions that had seemed so important earlier. He crawled under the covers, fully clothed and with damp hair, knowing he had much, *much* bigger things to worry about now.

The battered station wagon took the corner a little too sharply, its tires chirping against the curb. Will pulled to an abrupt stop in front of Claire's house, unbuckled his seat belt, and then stopped himself before he actually opened the car door. What was he doing? It wasn't even nine yet. He'd been afraid to call, worried about waking somebody up, but here he was, sitting in front of her house like some stupid stalker.

What am I going to do now? Send her thought rays?

Part of him wanted her to hear his thoughts and look out the window. But another part was worried that she'd look out and notice him sitting there in the ugly brown car in front of her house, hours early, and see him as the desperate loser he felt like.

Will looked at the house again and saw Claire at the open front door. He took a breath and got out, hoping with every step that he'd figure out exactly what he was supposed to say: Oh, my God? I'm so sorry?

"I saw the article in the paper," he began as he stepped

onto the porch. But then, as she started to cry, he just shut up and wrapped her in a hug.

Babies are only quiet when they sleep, Carrie decided. Teddy's wails put even Buddy's incessant whining to shame. She'd changed him, her supply of makeshift dish towel diapers running dangerously low. She'd fed him, though it didn't appear that Campbell's chicken noodle soup was his favorite; most of it ended up down the front of his shirt. She looked down at him hopefully when the crying stopped. But Teddy was merely catching his breath, readying himself for a whole new chorus.

She needed to get organized. *Babies are babies are babies*, she told herself. Kittens cry, and puppies howl. She'd seen it all before. How much harder could a human baby be? Carrie used the sofa cushions to create a soft pen on the living room floor. She didn't know whether Teddy was crawling yet, but she didn't want to take any chances.

"Mavis," she called. The dog came in from her hiding place under the kitchen table. "I need you to watch Teddy for a few minutes. I've got to do a load of laundry and bring the rest of those old clothes down from the attic." She needed to get to the store, too, but that would have to wait until Kurt showed up like he'd promised.

"Do they always cry like this?" Mavis asked, her voice morose.

"They cry all the time. *All* the time," said Penny, right at Mavis's heels, as usual. "I had these things where I used to live. They're loud for a while, but then they get bigger and they're a different kind of loud." She looked up at Carrie for approval.

"Can I have a treat?"

"Can you have a treat?" said Carrie.

Mavis's ears flew up like wings at the word.

"Did I hear *treat*?" Carl's voice was sleepy. Carrie had no idea how he managed to nap through all the noise.

"Treat! Treat!" yelled Buddy as he tore down the hallway. By the looks of the tissue that trailed behind him, she knew he'd been raiding the bathroom wastebasket again.

Belle swung through the cat door, complaining at the top of her lungs that *she* never got treats.

"Well," said Carrie, getting down the cardboard boxes of biscuits, "you would, if you stuck around more." She grabbed a handful.

"Take your biscuit in the living room," she told Mavis, directing her to sit next to the sofa cushions. Teddy reached for the big dog, drool running down his chin as he gurgled a laugh. Carrie passed out a treat to each of the other two dogs, and then turned on her heel. She had a lot of chores to do. And, she figured, hearing the wailing resume, not much time to finish them.

Kurt spent the morning staring at the ceiling of his room. Although he hated school, he actually wished he had to go today. He wouldn't even mind hanging out with Will during lunch—anything to escape the uneasy feeling that made his stomach gurgle and roll as if he actually *had* eaten a bad cheeseburger. He forced the worry from his mind, only to have it return twofold, his brain endlessly jabbering about all the bad things that could happen to him now.

Carrie had said she'd take care of it—the baby and anything else. He tried to think of other things, but the feeling of dread remained.

After his grandmother knocked on his door a few times, once to see whether she could get him some Pepto-Bismol and again to see whether he'd like some soup, he decided to get up. Saying he thought some fresh air would help, Kurt cautiously opened the front door. Finding no lines of uniformed officers yelling at him to put his hands up, he slipped outside. He blinked against the noon glare and headed back to Carrie's house. No matter what she said, this situation wasn't going to work. It just wasn't.

She didn't answer his knock, and no barking signaled his arrival. He knew Carrie was expecting him sometime today. The night before, she'd said she needed him to watch the baby while she went to the store. He tried the knob, found it unlocked, and walked into the living room. It was messier than he remembered.

"Hello?" he called softly. Didn't babies take naps? He crossed the room and entered the kitchen. Carl hopped down from the seat of one of the kitchen chairs, startling Kurt into a stifled scream. The purring animal curled around his legs in greeting. "Where *is* everybody?" he asked the cat, feeling a little silly. Carl bumped his head against Kurt's ankle as his answer.

"We were on a potty break," Carrie answered as she,

the baby, and the dogs came into the kitchen through the back door. She held the bare-bottomed baby at arm's length before setting him in the sink and turning on the tap. When water hit his pink skin, the infant at first looked shocked, then scrunched up his face for a full-throated bellow.

Kurt watched as Carrie picked up a cloth from the counter, squeezed some dish soap over it, and used it to scrub the rear of the crying child. "You'd think Teddy'd never had a bath before," she sighed. "Oh, he's just fine to do his business on the grass, but clean him up after"—she turned the water off and patted the baby dry with a dish towel—"and it's nothing but gripe, gripe—"

"Who's Teddy?" Kurt interrupted. "And what business does he do on the grass?" His mind was too full of the newspaper story and the worry that was chewing on the edges of his mind to truly process her words.

"Kurt, meet Teddy. Teddy, Kurt." Carrie now had the baby wrapped in what appeared to be a man's flannel shirt with the sleeves cut off. The baby's sobs subsided, and he began batting at Mavis's waving tail. "And his business is the same as the rest of our friends' here. My dish towel supply wasn't keeping up with Teddy's needs, so after he eats or plays or wakes up from a little nap, I get him outside right away. It's worked for every puppy I've ever raised, and it works for Teddy, too."

"Carrie," Kurt said, unsure of her potty-training method. But the bigger problem at hand far outweighed that twinge of doubt. "They're looking for him. The mini-mart was full of police and . . . " He dug the newspaper from his grandmother's recycling bin out of his backpack and showed her the photo on the front page.

"Will you hold him a minute, please?" Carrie asked, reaching for the paper. Kurt took Teddy and held him stiffly, smelling the lemon scent of the dish soap. Teddy settled in his arms, a contented, flannel-covered sack of potatoes.

"I figured there'd be a fuss at first," she said, scanning the story, then flipping to the third page, where it continued. "Don't worry, they'll forget about it soon enough. They always do. Maybe next time, that girl will do a better job of it." She closed the newspaper, tossed it on the kitchen table, and held out her arms for the baby.

"Forget about it?" Kurt shook his head. "They're not going to forget about it." He didn't want to hold the baby, and he didn't want to be having this conversation.

Carrie seemed to ignore his words as she grabbed the baby. "Today, we're going to go see Mother and Father at the cemetery. And I'd like you to come."

"Didn't you say you were low on milk?"

"I have plenty of lemonade in the fridge."

"Do babies drink lemonade?" Kurt asked. *They drink formula, right? Strained peaches, peas, all that kind of stuff.*

"It's full of vitamin C," Carrie assured Kurt, swiping her car keys off the counter.

"Carrie, we need to give him back," Kurt tried again. "We need to—"

"We need to *what*?" Carrie's voice was a screech, and the baby wrinkled up his face and started to wail. Kurt recoiled from both sounds.

"Put him back? Back to what? Dirty clothes? Empty parking lots?" Her voice became quieter with each question, and she jiggled the baby gently to stop his crying. Kurt felt his heart crawl up into his throat. "Back to what happened to you?" she asked, holding him in an icy blue gaze.

Kurt looked away. He wasn't sure. What if she was right? The worst part was, he didn't know whether he wanted her to be right or not.

"You worry too much," Carrie said.

Kurt felt Mavis's nose push into his hand. It felt good to have her there, and he rested his hand on her head. That was about the only thing he *was* sure of, the one thing in all the confusion—that Mavis was a good dog.

Carrie turned and walked toward the front door. "Let's go."

Kurt hesitated. A trip to see a couple of graves wasn't exactly his idea of an ideal Saturday. But then again, at this point, it had no chance of being even an okay day.

Carrie gave him a hard look. "Kurt, I need you to hold Teddy in the car. You don't want him to fly off the seat and get *hurt*, do you?"

"No, but . . . " He didn't finish his argument. He watched one of her eyebrows arch at his words. He didn't want her to get mad and yell again. He didn't think he could take it.

Kurt held the baby gingerly as he crouched on the floor of the big sedan for the short ride. Carrie kept her promise to take the corners carefully, so they were hardly jostled at all. He felt the car slow down, then heard the crunch of gravel under the tires.

"All clear," came Carrie's voice from the front seat. "I knew it would be, too. It's a rare day when I bump into anyone up here." She pulled the car to a stop. "But a couple of weeks from now, on Memorial Day, the place will be crawling with visitors." She opened the back door, lifting the baby out with a smile. "Listen to that peace and quiet," she said softly, then strode away from the car.

Kurt sat up and got out, stretching the life back into his legs. By the time he turned his head to take in his surroundings, Carrie and the baby were already halfway to the top of a grassy hill. He followed them through the headstones and was relieved to see that they were indeed alone. Most of the graves had an overgrown and untended look, and she was probably right about the lack of visitors.

But it was a different story when he caught up to Carrie. Fresh flowers filled the receptacles next to the twin headstones, and more grew from a large pot between them. The headstones stood out, too, with their ornate designs of animals wreathing the large block letters of Carrie's parents' names. He read the dates of their deaths, and saw that they both had died in the same year, Millicent first and then Theodore. *Theodore.* Kurt frowned at the name, puzzled at a thought that was just beyond his reach. He turned to Carrie, and she nodded at him.

"My father, Theodore, was a great man. And this one"—she nuzzled the side of the baby's neck, and he chortled with happiness—"has a long way to go before he fills his shoes. But he has time to grow into such a big name." She looked at Kurt, her eyes shining and a smile spreading across her face. "But I think Teddy will do just fine for now, don't you agree?"

Kurt felt his head bob in a nod. He didn't know what else to do. Then he looked at the blue sky, eager to lose himself for even a minute in the familiar comfort of the sparkles he always saw there.

Carrie hadn't felt this edgy in a very long time. Her nerves, her very innards, were taut as wires. Other wires, too, seemed to be sending buzzing, crackling electricity through her brain. Carl had absolutely nothing positive to say about Teddy. He blamed Carrie for the crying that filled every corner of the house, making it impossible to even think. Penny seemed to handle all of her stress by begging and constantly bombarded her with requests for just one more biscuit. Buddy kept busy, but his kind of busy usually involved shredding or chewing something of value into a worthless pile.

Teddy, in his sofa cushion pen, hadn't let up since Kurt left, hours earlier. The lemonade had not been at all to his liking, and Carrie had already opened the last can of soup in the house; he didn't seem to care for clam chowder, either. There was a break in the noise as Teddy caught a breath for a new round of wails. They were louder than any of the previous ones, and Carrie could not figure out how such a little baby could produce that sort of volume.

"Carrie, make it stop!" begged Mavis, planting herself at her feet.

Through the living room window, Carrie could see Belle glaring at her accusingly. She felt her vision go red. "Shut up, Mavis!" she screamed at the dog. "Not another word out of you!"

In response to Carrie's shout, Mavis snapped her mouth closed and the baby stopped crying. But the respite was short, and the wails started right back up again.

Penny crowded Carrie's feet, hoping for another biscuit, and the frazzled woman felt like crying herself as she went into the kitchen for the box. She took out two of the little bone-shaped cookies and handed one to the dachshund. But Mavis had slunk off to sulk. Carrie could still see Teddy from where she stood. His face was bright pink from crying, and his nose needed wiping again, along with his chin. That baby sure could drool. She looked at the biscuit in her hand once more before returning to the unhappy baby.

Teething?

Why didn't I do this earlier? Carrie knelt down and wrapped Teddy's pudgy fingers around the dog treat. He immediately stuck it in his mouth, and his sobs subsided to intermittent hiccups. His blue eyes, though still teary, were half closed in contentment. As Teddy gnawed ferociously on the biscuit, Carrie collapsed into her chair.

"I could have told you he was teething," Carl said snippily.

Carrie considered telling Carl to shut up, too. But at the moment, all she really wanted to do was listen to the welcome silence.

Usually, there was nothing to do on Sundays but hang around downtown, but today Kurt had no interest in being anywhere near there. He had no idea whether the cops were still camped out at the mini-mart, and he didn't want to find out. His grandmother seemed to talk of nothing but the missing baby. She kept going on about how terrible it all was, and what kind of monster would snatch a baby, and that poor girl, and how people who do such things should be locked up. Kurt had to get out, to get away from hearing anything more about it.

Taking his backpack, he left the house, thinking that at the very least he could look for some strays. Now, more than ever, he had a reason to leave this town far behind. And each forty bucks got him closer to doing that. Even though it felt worse and worse going back to Carrie's, especially because of the way she was acting, he needed the money and that's where he had to go to get it.

His footsteps on the sidewalk almost sounded like they were echoing his thoughts. *Forty bucks. Forty bucks. Forty bucks.* He kept his shoulders hunched up to his ears. It made him feel inconspicuous, and it reminded him of when he was younger, when he had imagined that he had super powers. One day, he pretended he could walk through walls. Another day, he fantasized he could fly. Finally, he'd decided that the super power he wanted most was to become invisible whenever he wanted. Hunching his shoulders was as close as he could get, he supposed, so he kept them high as he walked.

He couldn't stop thinking about the baby—or about Carrie, either. *She seems like she's taking care of him all right. She dresses him weird, but babies don't really care about clothes, do they? Her idea of baby food is strange, too, but the little kid looked okay, and he's clean, anyway.*

At least someone is taking care of him. Besides, she really seems to love him. She even named him after her dad.

The sound of his shoelace slapping against the sidewalk caught his attention, and Kurt knelt to tie it. And then he saw a flash of orange that made him hurry. He followed the big marmalade cat, gradually getting closer. The scruffy creature let him get near enough to almost reach out and scratch its ripped-up ears.

The runny stuff coming from its eye looked worse than before. The eye was now puffy and half shut against the sunlight. Kurt slowly lowered his backpack to the sidewalk so he could get out the animal carrier. He tossed a few dog treats at his feet for good measure, remembering how catnip had made this tomcat hiss last time.

As the cat moved forward to sniff at the treats, Kurt immediately pounced, wrapping it in a bear hug. Fending off the sharp claws and teeth of the enraged cat, he stuffed it into the carrier and zipped it shut. He looked furtively around, aware now that he hadn't even checked to see whether the coast was clear. But the street was empty, and he felt almost light-headed with relief. Hoisting his backpack on his shoulder and gripping the carrier handle, he walked swiftly away, thinking of the money the cat would bring him, his footsteps accompanied by the barking of dogs in backyards. *Forty bucks. Forty bucks. Forty bucks.* Kurt gave the side of the carrier a reassuring pat.

"Excuse me."

Kurt froze at the sound of the man's voice over his shoulder. The old man stood only a few feet away. Where had he come from? He hadn't been there a moment before.

No one had been there. Kurt thought about dumping the carrier and taking off. There was no way that old guy could catch him, but Kurt's feet felt nailed to the pavement.

"I, I . . . " he began, wondering how he was going to explain taking someone's cat, probably this guy's.

The man thrust a sheet of paper at him. "Reward," it said, with the picture from the newspaper, the picture of Teddy, staring from the photocopy. "Have you seen this baby? He's my grandson." Kurt noticed that the man wasn't really that old. It probably was worry that made him appear that way.

"No," Kurt squeaked. There was barely enough air left in his lungs to breathe, let alone speak.

"Would you take it with you anyway, just in case?" The man pressed the sheet into Kurt's free hand.

Kurt nodded wordlessly, watching the man go up the walk to leave a flyer on the doorstep of the next house.

"Thanks," the man said over his shoulder.

Kurt didn't answer, but headed quickly toward Carrie's. His heart dropped, however, when he remembered that she had specifically told him not to come today, that she needed some quiet time. He hadn't felt too bad about that. A day of not seeing the baby might mean a day of not thinking about him, either. Unfortunately, it hadn't worked out that way, because whenever he closed his eyes, the only thing he saw was the baby's face.

Should he let the cat go? He was pretty sure he'd never be able to catch it again, and its eye looked real bad. He would just have to figure out a way to hide it from his grandmother and then take it to Carrie's on Monday. He headed home as fast as he could while carrying the cat, trying not to jostle it. It was mad as anything already; no need to make it any more so.

Before Kurt walked in the front door, he went around to the side and opened his bedroom window to put the cat inside. He'd explain it to his grandmother if he had to. It was only going to have to stay there until tomorrow anyway, and if he was careful, he wouldn't even have to say anything about it.

As he walked in the front door, a news break was blaring from the television, and once again, Kurt saw the picture of the baby on the screen, along with the oversized caption: LOCAL INFANT KIDNAPPED.

His grandmother wasn't in the room, and unable to bear seeing the image for another second, Kurt reached out to shut it off, only then noticing that he still held the flyer with the baby's picture on it. He hurriedly stuffed the paper in his pocket, vowing to rip it to shreds and flush it down the toilet as soon as he had the chance.

With the noise of the television gone, Kurt heard his grandmother's voice in the kitchen. He followed the sound and found her on the telephone.

"Here he is, John. He just walked in the door." It was his father. She extended the phone to Kurt, but he didn't take it. He let his backpack fall to the floor instead, using the time to think about what he'd say to his dad.

His grandmother put her hand over the mouthpiece. "Go on," she urged. "He wants to talk to you." She put the telephone in his hand. "Here."

"Hello?" Kurt was surprised to hear his voice sound almost normal.

"Kurt! It's good to hear your voice. You been minding your grandmother?" His father's words boomed through the phone, and Kurt closed his eyes to picture the big man on the other end.

"Yeah."

"So, tell me the news. How's school working out for you? I bet it hasn't changed much since I went there. Say, is old Iron Butt still around?"

"Iron Shorts."

"Yeah, well, Irons was already old and mean as sin when I was a kid. I'd hate to know what he's like now."

"The same." *Is this what he called for, to talk about a teacher?* There was a moment of dead air, when neither of them spoke.

"You're working, too, I hear." His father had switched to an even more upbeat tone. "That's good, keeping yourself out of trouble."

Kurt felt a sob rise in his chest. His dad had no idea about trouble. He willed the tears behind his closed lids to stop. "I want to get out of here, Dad."

There were another few seconds of silence before his father spoke again. "Now, Kurt, your grandmother told me that she explained the deal to you. When school gets out for the summer, then you can come."

"You just don't want me there because you got married," Kurt shot back. The accusation raced over the line, and his dad was silent again.

"Your grandmother told me you know about that now, too. I was going to tell you, but it never felt like the right time." His tone brightened. "But Marion's great, and you'll love the heck out of her."

"What about Mom?" *I want to get out of here. If I'm not going with you, then I'll get her to take me*, Kurt thought. But he knew it was probably the stupidest thought he'd ever had.

"Your mom?" His dad's voice sounded puzzled, and Kurt was glad his dad didn't know what else he'd been thinking just then.

"You know your mom. She'll land on her feet. She always does."

"Dad?" Kurt all of a sudden felt old, way older than the man who had given him the flyer, older than his grandmother, even. He felt older than anyone he could think of.

"What is it, son?"

I don't know what to do here, Dad. There's a whole lot of trouble here that I don't know how to fix. Carrie says it's the right thing, but everyone told me I did the right thing to Mark, too. But how can what I did to him really be the right thing? How can anyone tell? What should I do, Dad? Tell me what to do.

"Grandma wants to talk to you." Kurt handed the phone over and walked down the hallway to his room, closing the door behind him. He thought about taking the cat over to Carrie's now, even if she didn't want him there, but he couldn't summon the energy. And he wasn't sure he was up to seeing the baby, either. Being confronted by his face everywhere he went, from the newspaper to flyers to the television screen, was bad enough. It wasn't like he was going to need the forty dollars for the cat today, anyway. Tomorrow would be soon enough.

He opened the carrier, but now the wary cat stayed put

inside. Kurt shrugged, leaving it open anyway, and took his mother's letter from its place under the piece of petrified wood. He sat on the edge of the bed and carefully unfolded it. The paper was thin from so much unfolding and refolding, and he probably could recite the letter by heart. But even so, he sat on his bed and reread it.

Even before the first class, word had already spread through the school about Claire's cousin's baby, and Will overheard pieces of conversation as he walked through the halls. Some said Lydia had sold her baby to some foreign couple for millions. She and her baby were victims of some secret cult. It was taken by a serial killer, a meth head, or even a devil worshiper. Or the baby wasn't gone at all, and Lydia just wanted the attention.

Will brushed past the groups and headed for Claire's locker, but he didn't find her there. He looked through the doorway of her first-period classroom and didn't see her there, either.

At noon in the library, Will looked up when he sensed someone standing next to him, expecting to see Kurt. Instead, he was surprised to see a dark-haired man in a sport coat. *That is the ugliest tie I've ever seen*, he thought. *Paisley?* He tasted mayonnaise at the word *paisley* and wished he had a sandwich. His stomach growled in agreement.

"Are you Will? Will Miller?" the man asked.

Will said yes, trying not to stare at the gaudy splotches of color on the tie hanging from the guy's neck.

"I'm Detective Reuben. Do you have a minute?"

Will nodded and accepted the policeman's handshake, aware that his palms were starting to sweat. *Why do I need to feel nervous?* But he did, in the same way he hated having a squad car follow his station wagon, even when he knew he wasn't doing anything wrong. *It's not like I'm my brother.*

"You were at the Lemay residence last Thursday?"

"Lemay?" Will asked. "Claire's house?"

The policeman nodded. "Did you notice anything out of the ordinary at the party you attended there?"

Will wiped his palms on his pants legs. "Well, there were people there wearing ducks on their heads."

Detective Reuben's face remained serious as he waited for Will to elaborate. "They were giving out little paper hats, and they looked like ducks. . . . " Will's voice trailed off.

"You heard no offhand comments or anything that struck you as odd?" The detective waited for Will's response.

Will swallowed, feeling his Adam's apple move. He didn't dare give another smart-ass answer. He shook his head. "No. Nothing that I can think of."

The detective stood and reached again into his sport coat to hand Will a business card. "Thank you for your time, Will. If you think of anything, anything at all, please give me a call."

Will looked past the man to see Kurt standing several feet away. He didn't come closer until the cop was gone.

"Ugly tie, huh?" asked Will, breathing a little easier

now that the detective was gone. Kurt sat down, but didn't answer.

Will's relief at having Kurt show up again, even after his stupid remark, faded at the sight of the thin sheen of sweat over the kid's almost gray face. "Kurt, are you feeling all right?" he asked, concerned that there might really be something wrong with him. *And man, do you have dark circles under your eyes.*

"I'm fine."

"Okay." Will tipped back in his chair a bit. *Just don't breathe on me.* "So today, I want you to write a two-paragraph essay. It can be about anything you want, but you have to use the same synonyms and antonyms you gave me last week." Will slid the paper from Friday across his desk. "Here."

Kurt started writing, and Will again thought about phoning Claire. But he'd already left her two messages. *If she wants to talk to me, she knows how to get a hold of me.*

He closed his eyes for a moment, thinking how much he'd like to ask her to go to a movie, get pizza, anything. He worried that maybe he had said something wrong the last time he saw her. He wished things could go back to the way they were only a couple of days ago.

Kurt nudged his shoulder. "I'm done."

Will took the piece of notebook paper and glanced at the two-paragraph essay. The kid's handwriting hurt his eyes.

It is difficult to ignore a situation when someone isn't doing their job. We could disregard their actions and tune-

*out what they're doing, but that would be wrong. Care-
lessness is something that can't be condoned.*

Will nodded at that line.

*Inattentiveness should not be excused, either. We must
live our lives, not as a bad mother, but as someone that is
just trying to help.*

Will put the piece of paper down, feeling kind of sorry
for the kid. This whole bad mother thing must be a big deal
to him. That was an understatement, considering Kurt's reaction last time. The kidnapping probably didn't help, either. And now he's sick. This kid really can't catch a break.

I think you're nice. That's what Claire had said. He
wanted her to keep thinking that. He was going to do everything he could to make her keep thinking that way.

"Kurt," he said. The boy looked up at him. "I thought
I was here to help you with your grades. But I can see that
you haven't been straight with me."

Kurt met his gaze with a look of panic.

Will continued quickly. *He really is freaked out.* "You
haven't shown me what you can really do until now. This is
good." He tapped the edge of the notebook paper. "Now I
know you can do the work. You just have to actually do it."
Will saw Kurt relax a little, then the boy nodded, his pale
face unreadable again.

"Okay, now try this—and don't worry, it's no big
deal," Will added as the kid's shoulders slumped. "It's just
a short story, a very short story. You pick the subject, any-

thing you want." Will was tempted to add something about making the handwriting a little neater, but decided against it. He had gotten the kid to at least be willing to write and hadn't made any stupid remarks about mothers this time. *Why ruin it by criticizing his handwriting?*

"Okay," said Kurt, his pencil already moving across the paper.

~

"Still not talking to me, Mavis?" Carrie waved the dog biscuit in front of the big German shepherd's long nose, but got no response.

"Me! Give it to me, Carrie!" Penny stood up, prairie dog fashion, her brown eyes glued to the treat. Buddy held an identical pose beside her.

"No more for either one of you. You're both going to get fat." She handed the biscuit to Teddy, who immediately shoved it between his gums. She ran her fingers through her tangled hair, wondering idly when her own last meal had been, then was thrilled to discover it didn't matter. When she was on, really on, hunger had no power over her.

Carrie knew the lemonade was finally gone and the last can of clam chowder, too—when was that? Yesterday? The day before? She looked down and saw that her shirt was stained, and she couldn't quite remember how long she'd been wearing it. The days all seemed to run together whenever she didn't sleep.

"How do you expect us to get fat when you don't feed us?" Carl's yowl ripped through the kitchen.

Carrie turned to glare at the three-legged cat. "What do you mean, I don't feed you? Of course I feed you."

"Not today." Penny paced back and forth beneath the biscuit box on the counter.

"And not yesterday, either." Carl's ears were set back flat against his head. "Belle left last night. Maybe I should have gone with her."

Carrie glanced down at the cat door and quickly fastened it shut.

"I take good care of you!" she shouted as she straightened up, startling Teddy into another fit of crying. The suit jacket she'd split down the middle as another improvised diaper suddenly grew wet and warm. Damn! That was the third time today she'd been late getting him outside to go potty.

"Well, if it's anything like how you took care of your friends up there on the hill, I'd rather take my chances with Belle," Carl sneered.

Carrie handed Teddy another biscuit to hold in his other hand, and the crying stopped. She plopped his bare bottom in the kitchen sink to rinse him off.

"Whatever, Carl. You never listen to me, anyway." She began to fill the sink with water, turning a deaf ear to Teddy's wails and the whines of the animals.

Kurt's stomach had been in a knot since he overheard Will and the cop talking about the baby. It took him only a couple of steps from the library door before he knew he was going to hurl. The boy's bathroom was empty, and he had the presence of mind to be grateful, even through the actual act of losing his breakfast.

Leaving the stall, he stopped by the sink to wash his hands and throw some water on his face. He glanced in the mirror, catching sight of his worried expression, and thought of the baby's grandfather. He knew he had to get the baby back from Carrie. There was no way they were going to stop looking for it, no matter what Carrie said. Besides, the way he was acting, he might as well be wearing a tee shirt with "I Stole the Baby" written on it. He turned off the water.

Two boys, probably a year older, came through the door.

"Stinks in here," said one, wrinkling his nose and staring at him.

"Yeah, smells like puke," said the other.

Kurt shrugged and moved toward the exit.

"Did you do it?" The bigger one blocked his way.

"I gotta go." Kurt kept his eyes and head down, hoping they'd let him go.

The one nearer to Kurt grabbed his arm, just like Carrie had—and just like Mark had. He held it in a painful grip and pulled Kurt's face up close to his. He was now so close that Kurt could smell his breath.

"Let me go." Kurt forced his voice as low as he could manage, but it still sounded like a squeak to him.

"Let me go." The other boy, who had been keeping an eye on the door, echoed Kurt's words in a girlish falsetto.

The grip on his arm grew tighter, the boy's nails digging through Kurt's sleeve and into the tender skin of his scars. Kurt's ears began to fill with a rushing sound, and suddenly it wasn't the boy who was holding him anymore.

"Let me go!" he'd raged. His mom stood in a corner of the living room, the side of her face a shade of red that Kurt knew would soon be turning purple.

Mark laughed and tightened his grip, lifting Kurt up onto his toes.

"Let him go, Mark." His mother's voice was muffled, and Kurt wondered whether this time Mark had finally broken her jaw. "Let him go, Mark," she repeated.

Mark moved the cigarette to the side of his mouth as he repeated Kurt's mother's words, mocking her. But then Kurt struck out at him with his free arm, landing a blow to the side of Mark's head. Mark shifted, wrapping a meaty hand around both of Kurt's wrists. "You little SOB!"

Kurt watched him take the cigarette from his lips, hold it between thumb and forefinger, and then his mother's screams and the pain on his arm became one.

"Let me go!" Kurt's scream ripped through the boy's bathroom.

"Let him go!" Kurt looked up to see Will standing at the door.

"Dude. We were just messin' with him." The older boy released his grip, and Kurt collapsed against the side of the sink. They laughed on their way out of the restroom. Embarrassed, humiliated, and enraged, Kurt brushed past Will and headed to his next class. Three more classes, he thought, trying to breathe normally. He had almost three hours to come up with a way to make Carrie give the baby back.

When the dismissal bell rang, Kurt still had no plan other than delivering the orange tabby. He jogged home, hoping that his grandmother hadn't found the cat. He'd left the lid of a shoebox filled with shredded newspaper as a makeshift litter box and prayed the big tom figured out how he should use it.

The house seemed quiet when he walked in the front door, but he found his grandmother waiting for him at the kitchen table.

"Is there something you want to tell me, honey?" she asked. She took a drag off her cigarette.

Kurt's nerves were stretched as far as they could go. Yes, there was something he wanted to tell her—probably more than she ever wanted to know.

"What do you mean?" he finally managed to ask.

"Your orange roommate, Kurt." His grandmother stubbed out her smoke. "Next time, pick friends with better manners, okay?"

"Orange?" Kurt wanted to shriek the question.

"Your cat did his business on the rug, Kurt. If you want a pet, *tell* me. We'll get a proper litter box and some real pet food. Tuna fish is too expensive to be feeding a cat."

"It's not mine," he said, taking a deep enough breath to start his brain working again. "I'm taking care of it for the lady I'm working for."

"You're taking it back, then?"

"Yeah. I'm sorry. I'll clean up the mess before I leave."

His grandmother reached out to gently wrap her fingers around his wrist and pulled him toward her. "All taken care of, honey. Sit down for a minute, though, okay?"

Kurt sat down opposite her, his body tense and ready to leave as soon as she was finished.

"I talked to your mom today."

Kurt's attention was now completely on his grandmother. "About dad getting married?" he asked.

She shook her head. "No, not really. We talked more about her—and about you, too."

"Yeah, right," he began, but couldn't summon up the venom needed to make a nasty remark.

"I've invited her to stay with me when she gets out."

"She's going to *live* here?" Kurt took careful breaths, trying to comprehend it.

"For a little while. Just until she gets back on her feet."

"Well, I should be gone by the time she gets here," Kurt said. "I'll be at my dad's or"—he stopped—"wherever."

"I was hoping you'd stay for a few extra days, maybe even a week. It would be good for her." His grandmother put her hand on his arm again, her gentle touch instantly quieting the itch of his scars. "I think it might be good for you, too."

Kurt shook his head, but she continued to hold his gaze. "I don't know," he said, finally.

She gave his arm a pat and smiled. "Think about it."

He got up to retrieve the cat from his room. "Okay, Grandma."

He hauled the carrier down the street as he headed to Carrie's house, the cat bumping angrily against its sides. A flash of sunlight glinted off the bumper of an old Volkswagen Beetle as it buzzed by, making Kurt remember the shooting star he'd seen last week and the memory of his mother's voice urging him to make a wish. He hadn't bothered last week, but as he moved steadily through the heat of the afternoon, he sure was ready to make a wish now.

Will left another message for Claire and passed by her house as he drove home from school, but he didn't see her. He wanted so badly to ask her to go for a run. *It might get her mind off things, right?* But he knew it was more about wanting to be with her than concern for her peace of mind. He did care and hoped she was okay; that was true. He wondered whether there was any news about the baby, and he thought back to the happy faces at the baby shower, realizing he hadn't even given the family a thought. They'd all been so nice to him, too.

I am a jerk. I am just like my brother. He hit the accelerator. *Jerk.*

Even though it was a hot afternoon, Will decided to try a longer run. He'd been considering it, and sore legs and side stitches might be just the thing to clear his mind. He wound his way through the downtown area, passing the posters of Lydia's baby and flyers for lost pets that covered every telephone pole. Later, the sidewalks turned to gravel, and Will was happy to leave it all behind for a while as he found himself on the narrow shoulder of a county road.

As the yards and miles passed beneath his feet, the scene in the bathroom today wouldn't leave him. Sure, he knew underclassmen risked a hassle if they got caught there, but this was more than that, and Will couldn't help thinking about that last day at the grocery store.

His brother had gotten worse—a lot worse. But Will couldn't remember whether it had been only days or weeks. He'd become more insistent about demanding money from their mom. And the more she said no, the more he insisted.

Will had driven his mom to the store. She liked the pharmacist there, and she had coupons for groceries, too. If he'd seen his brother drive up, would he have said something to him? Would he have tried to stop him? He hadn't done a thing when his brother showed up in the cereal aisle, acting like a crazy man, yelling and waving his arms.

Had it occurred to Will to push his brother back? Had he even thought to have someone call 911 or let someone know they needed help?

Will didn't remember thinking about doing any of it. All he remembered was standing there, watching his mother yell back at his brother. His brother had shoved their mother, and she fell backward, hitting her head on the shelves of cans behind her and then lying motionless on the supermarket floor. His brother had run out, and Will had stayed with their mom, her head in his lap. But he didn't remember much more after that.

And then there was the hospital. He remembered better what the doctors had told him there. But by then, it didn't really matter much, did it?

The heat from the asphalt combined with the sun beating down on the back of Will's neck as he kept his steady pace past the sparse houses and the fields of cows, sheep, and occasional horses. The sound of birds and insects was the only accompaniment to the rhythm of his steps, and since there was no barking, he supposed that the farm dogs were all lying low in the shade.

A figure emerged ahead of him as he rounded a bend, shimmering in the heated air. Will slowed a bit, recognizing the combined shapes of boy and carrier. *That's funny. He looks like he's carrying a purse.* He'd seen Kurt lugging that thing around town last week and had thought it looked strange then, too. *What's he doing all the way out here?* Will slowed to a walk and then stopped altogether as Kurt made a right into a graveled driveway. He forced himself to count to 10 before resuming his run, trying to muffle his footsteps. He reached the driveway in time to see Kurt walk up the steps of the wide porch and then walk in without even knocking.

Will ran for another hundred yards or so, then turned around to head back home. But this time he saw nothing else as he passed the house.

"Put him in the bathroom," Carrie ordered when she saw the marmalade cat glaring at her through the mesh of the carrier. The cat spat something unintelligible at her. "And make sure the door's shut," she added. There was no way she was letting that cat get away again.

Buddy and Penny flanked Kurt as he wandered back into the living room, and Carrie watched him stoop down to greet Teddy in his sofa-cushion playpen. But seeing the look on his face when he straightened up, she knew something was wrong.

"Carrie, there's posters all over town for him. I've seen him on the news. And there was a *cop* at my school today!"

Carrie sighed in irritation. Her eyes felt hot and dry, and she tried to blink away the sand. "I know that, Kurt. I was in town at the store today. I told you there would be a fuss, and that it'd all blow over before long."

"I'm hungry," said Buddy.

"Hungry, hungry, hungry." Penny spun around and around at Carrie's feet.

"I'll feed you when Mavis says pretty please," Carrie snapped. But Mavis and Carl stared silently at her from the kitchen doorway.

"What did you say?" Kurt's voice drowned out the dogs' for a moment.

"I said it will blow over."

The boy stood there stubbornly—at least, that's how it looked to her. "How did you get to the store?" he asked.

Carrie walked over to pick up Teddy. *I must be getting stronger*, she thought. *He's feeling lighter all the time*. She tucked the plaid shirt over his bare bottom. "It's called a car, Kurt. It's an amazing invention."

"No, I mean who watched Teddy while you were at the store?"

"Mavis. But don't ask her anything. She's not talking to anybody these days."

"The *dog* watched the baby?"

Carrie reached up and rubbed her eyes. They felt like two embers stuck in her head. "He was fine. He was sleeping. You didn't seem to think he was so fine where he was before, did you? But now you've changed your mind? You think that being carted all over town and left in parking lots and having smoke forced down his lungs is better for him than having a nice safe nap with Mavis watching him?"

The boy was silent, but he remained standing where he was.

"Do you actually think"—Carrie could feel the knife-edge in her voice, but she needed it now—"that if anyone knew you were responsible for taking a baby"—she watched his eyes grow wide, his mouth a vacant oval—"they'd let you, a *kidnapper*, leave this town? Ever?"

The boy stood still and silent. *If only that worked with Carl*, she thought.

"Here," Carrie said. She made her voice kinder now. It looked like she'd finally gotten the boy to listen. "I'll get you your money for the cat."

Carrie thrust the baby at Kurt and turned to get her purse, but the sound of a gag and a cough made her turn back around. A stream of vomit erupted from the baby, covering the fronts of both Kurt's and Teddy's clothes.

"Oh, god." Kurt's voice was almost a gag.

"Oh, it's just a little barf." Impatiently, Carrie whipped Teddy from Kurt's arms and peeled the soiled shirt off the baby. The placid baby didn't seem the slightest bit bothered by the mess. "Give me your shirt, too, Kurt. I'll take care of it." When the boy hesitated, she snorted. "I've already *seen* your arm. I know you have those scars." So he handed her the long-sleeved shirt that he always wore over his tee shirts. "There's one thing you better get straight in this life, Kurt. *Everyone* has scars. Now, do you mind if I write you a check? I seem to have spent the last of my cash."

~

"Oh, god." Kurt could smell the barf before he could feel it hit his shirt. Brown and chunky, it reminded him of the canned cat food his mother had fed his kitten. He struggled to retain his stomach's contents.

"Oh, it's just a little barf," Carrie said.

A little hurricane, a little nuclear war. A little bit of bad was still bad. But then, scars or not, he let her have his shirt.

But the barf wasn't as bad as what Carrie had said. And the worst part was, he knew it was true. If anyone found out he'd had anything to do with the baby's kidnapping, they'd put him away—maybe forever. He'd been shocked when they let him go after what happened with Mark. This time, there wouldn't be any second chances.

So what now? Even though Carrie made it sound like she had everything under control, she didn't look too good. She was wearing the same shirt as on Saturday, and by the looks of the stains down the front, she hadn't washed it since then. And what was the deal with her hair? It looked like a Halloween wig.

Even the animals seemed weird now. They usually mobbed him as soon as he was in the door, but today, the little ones barely came up to him, and Mavis and the three-legged cat kept their distance. Carrie hadn't been letting them out enough, either. He had seen a couple of piles of dog poop right next to the back door.

Kurt kicked a stone along as he walked back to town. The late afternoon sun beat down on his bare arms, making him feel even more naked. Since the day Mark had burned him with that glowing cigarette, he'd always worn that shirt. At first, he'd even slept in it. But looking down at the circles of pink and puckered skin, he knew he'd rather expose them than wear that stinking, barf-covered shirt.

Could she be right? Would it all blow over? Carrie seemed so sure, and he wanted now more than ever to believe her.

Kurt recalled how he had felt seeing the baby in a haze of smoke in town and at the park. He remembered how hard it had been, hearing him cry all alone on the sidewalk outside the fast-food restaurant and then sitting in the stroller at the mini-mart parking lot.

Carrie had taken the baby for a reason. Why was it so hard for him to remember that?

Then he pictured that grandfather's face, lined and full of worry. It reminded him of how his own grandmother had looked when he'd arrived at her house a few months earlier. She'd been worried about him and had said so.

His puzzling over whether he was right to keep Carrie's secret seemed to blur again. Even if he'd asked his dad about this situation, would he have had the answer? Kurt kicked the stone into the gutter as he reached the main drag. Then a beat-up station wagon pulled up beside him.

"Hey, Kurt," came a familiar voice, and he saw Will leaning out the window on the passenger side.

Man, does this guy live here? I keep seeing him here all the time, shoveling in the food, Kurt thought.

"I'm sick of cooking. I think I'm going to eat here every night," Will said through the window.

156

"Yeah, it's good," Kurt replied. After having Will witness his humiliation in the bathroom earlier that day, Kurt wanted to get as far away from him as possible.

"Then come on in. I'll buy."

Kurt hesitated. But Will *had* told the a-holes in the bathroom to get lost. How many other people had done that for him lately? And anyway, having some company, even of a senior he hardly knew, was better than being stuck alone with the confusion of his thoughts. He could go home, but his grandmother would want to talk more about his mom. And Kurt wasn't ready for that—at least not yet.

"I guess I could eat some fries," Kurt conceded, jamming his hands into the pockets of his jeans to keep the insides of his arms pressed tight against his body and out of sight.

They walked in together and went up to the counter to order. Kurt spent an endless minute regarding the baby's face on a flyer posted next to the cash register, then Will picked up their plastic order number and Kurt followed him to the nearest empty table. Sitting down on the hard booth seat, he pulled his hands from his pockets but kept his scarred arm hidden below the edge of the tabletop. He could still see the picture of the baby from their table.

Will sat down heavily across from him and rubbed his forehead. "It's creepy, isn't it?"

"What?" Kurt asked. Two girls walked past their table, one stealing a glance at Will. The other looked at Kurt with a questioning stare.

Will looked back at him, surprised. "The Noah Lemay thing."

157

"Noah?" Kurt asked. He didn't know any Noah.

"The baby." Will raised his brows, then pointed toward the counter and the poster. He stared at Kurt as if he saw three eyeballs in his head. That's when Kurt realized with a shock that he'd never even considered that the baby had a real name. Before he was Teddy, he'd just been "it" or "that baby." *The dirty baby. The crying baby. The smoky baby. The baby left out all alone, where anyone could have grabbed it.*

"I kind of know the family." Will waited as the counter girl set two trays on the table and left. "But how weird is that? A baby being stolen? That's enough to devastate anybody."

Devastate: ruin, demolish, destroy. The synonyms raced through Kurt's head.

When Kurt heard Mark start up that last day, he'd had enough and was planning to demolish, ruin, and destroy the guy once and for all. Kurt took the screwdriver from the utility drawer in the kitchen, not to scare him, but to use it.

"Get out of here, Mark!" his mother screamed, and Kurt heard the thud as she hit the living room wall. He stuck the pointy screwdriver in his back pocket and ran into the room, but Mark had him by the arm before he could reach his mom. Then came the cigarette and the screaming—his mom's and his own—that filled him until he couldn't listen to it anymore. The only way to make it all stop—to make it quiet again—was to reach into his back pocket and . . .

The splattering sound made by a little girl spilling her drink on the floor brought Kurt back from the memory. He took a fry from the basket and nibbled at it, glad to have his mind back at the restaurant again.

158

"Bummer," Will said as he noticed the little girl's predicament. He pulled his burger toward him but didn't take a bite. "I can't imagine having my kid disappear. It'd be horrible not knowing if you'd ever see him again."

Kurt hadn't seen his mother again after that day. The police separated them right away, not even letting them see each other at the hospital. Then Kurt had cooled his heels at the police station and then in juvie, until his dad came to get him. He'd asked his dad about his mom once, but was answered only with silence. And then he'd stopped asking.

"Hey, I saw you after school today." Will spoke through the first bite of his burger. He swallowed and wiped his mouth.

"Sure, you saw me here," Kurt replied. *Just when I thought this guy could border on normal.*

"No, earlier. I was on a run and saw you going to somebody's house. You were carrying some kind of suitcase thing."

The French fry in Kurt's mouth turned to dirt. "I work for a lady out there," he said, over the pounding of his heart. "I was just bringing her something. Something she wanted." He stood up. "I better go. My grandmother's waiting for me."

Kurt saw Will's eyes widen, and it looked like he was going to say something else. But Kurt didn't give him a chance. He turned on his heel and was out the door, walking quickly until it was safe to run.

Will stared in shock at the round, red scars on Kurt's arm. *Those have got to be from a cigarette.* He'd thought there was something different about the kid's appearance when he spotted him in the parking lot. Now those angry marks made him realize that Kurt wasn't wearing his usual long-sleeved shirt. Will had never seen him without it.

He took a breath and was about to tell him to wait, to stay for a minute. He wanted to ask him what had happened. But Kurt was already gone, taking his secrets with him.

Will returned to his burger, then wiped his mouth on a paper napkin that somehow fell through his fingertips. Bending to retrieve it, another slip of paper caught his eye. It was a check made out to Kurt. He picked it up and saw that it was from Carrie Williams. The name looked familiar, somehow. Then he realized that the address was probably for the farmhouse where he had seen Kurt during his run this afternoon.

He lost interest in the remnants of his hamburger as he attempted to revive foggy memories that at last bobbed up to the surface. *That story my mom told me.* As a kid, he had had nightmares about it.

His mother had gone to school with Carrie Williams. She said Carrie was pretty but weird. In fact, she called her odd. But the story his mom told him about her wasn't odd. It was downright horrible.

First, her parents had died a few months apart—right after she and Carrie graduated from high school. And then Carrie just dropped out of sight.

She knew Carrie had a whole bunch of dogs and cats

at her place, and she spent most of her time taking care of them. So people rarely saw her in town, and it wasn't anything unusual at first. But after a couple of weeks, Will's uncle went over to check on her. As he stepped up onto the porch, the first thing he noticed was the smell.

This was the part that had totally freaked Will out as a kid, and he wondered why his mother had even told him about it when he was so young. This was the kind of thing his brother would have wanted to hear. Was his brother even there, then? Will couldn't remember.

Anyway, his uncle had found the front door unlocked, and when he went inside, he'd never smelled anything like it. The living room, the kitchen, the hallway, and the bathroom were filled with dead or almost dead animals. He found Carrie in her parents' bedroom. She was dirty, wouldn't talk, and was only skin and bones. The ambulance came. Then no one saw Carrie Williams for a long time after that.

Will's uncle had been the Williamses' neighbor for years, so he took it upon himself to bury all the bodies of the animals on the hill behind the house beside the existing wooden crosses. Carrie may have been crazy, but she was still his friend's daughter and those poor creatures had meant the world to her. Not knowing any of their names, he'd written simply "brown dog" or "gray striped cat" on some shingles from his barn. He figured she'd know who was who when she got back.

Will folded the check and stuck it in his pocket, musing. He hadn't thought about that story for years. His aunt and uncle had moved away, and he hadn't realized that Crazy Carrie still lived in that house.

What could Kurt possibly be doing over there? He said he was bringing her something. Something in a suitcase? He must have had something for her last week, too, when Will saw him carrying the same bag.

He took a sip from his shake, but heard the gurgle of an empty cup. Crumpling the empty wrappers, he threw everything into the trash on his way out the door, including Kurt's uneaten French fries.

So weird. With that word, the taste of his supper was eclipsed by a flood of banana, sickeningly sweet and over-ripe.

Carrie had had little use for television in the past, but she now found the noise helpful. For one thing, it kept Teddy quiet. It also drowned out the animals' yammering. They were always complaining about something, and even the birdsong from the yard seemed to pick at her. Only Mavis kept her thoughts to herself now. Well, thought Carrie, *she's making her own bed then, isn't she? Until she gets it into her head to say please, they all can wait for their dinner.*

"Carrie. Carrie!" Carl's raspy voice diverted her attention from the dish towels she was resorting.

"What do you want, Carl?" She didn't look at him. She was sick of being criticized by the gray cat.

Carl set himself in the middle of the freshly folded towels. *Damn*, now she would have to recount and refold them all over again.

"Carrie, take your pills."

"No." She yanked a stack of towels from under him.

"Please, Carrie. I've seen you bad before, but not like this. If you take your pills, you'll get better again."

"I'm not crazy, Carl." Carrie counted as she folded. The towels with eight stripes went to the left, and they absolutely had to be folded in that precise way.

"If you took your pills, you'd feed us. And you'd let us out."

Carrie grabbed a plaid towel, trying to remember the correct direction of stripes she was supposed to count on these. *Oh, yes, lengthwise.* She refolded it in record time, then started a new pile of six.

"It's up to Mavis when you get fed, so go talk to her. And I'm not letting you out. I heard you, Buddy, and Penny talking. You're all going to leave."

"Just feed us, Carrie." Carl pleaded.

Carrie walked over to the television and increased the volume. She glanced at the red-cheeked Teddy in his circle of cushions and noticed the puddle beneath him. But since he was sound asleep, she didn't want to bother him. Bless his heart, he'd been sleeping almost nonstop the whole day. What a good baby he was! She kicked at Carl, and as he stalked away, she went back to folding and refolding the towels.

Kurt stood at the front door of his grandmother's house, listening to the blare of the TV. He grabbed the doorknob, but then changed his mind. He couldn't just go in there and talk to her and act like nothing was wrong. He couldn't sit there and eat dinner, knowing there was a world of people looking for that baby *and probably looking for me*. He turned around to leave.

And now Will had seen him at Carrie's. It wouldn't be long before someone else figured out the rest. They could do whatever they wanted to him. It couldn't be worse than living with this. He was going back to Carrie's, and this time he wasn't leaving without Noah.

The sun was low in the sky, and the golden light illuminating the buildings in town would normally make him stop just to look. But it felt more like a glare now, exposing him and his misdeeds to the world. He walked faster, aware of his backpack with the carrier inside bumping against him. He rounded a corner, and there was Lydia.

But she wasn't with her friends this time. And there was no cigarette hanging from her mouth, no snarky smile. She was with the man who had given him the flyer earlier, the one who said he was the baby's grandfather. *This must be Lydia's dad*. The man held Lydia's hand, while a woman *(Maybe her mom?)* had her arm around Lydia's shoulder. Lydia's eyes were red and almost swollen shut, and her parents looked very tired.

The family walked past him. And even though they never looked at him, Kurt shrank against the building. He waited until there was some distance between them before continuing on. Picking up his pace now, he stayed in the shadows and avoided the golden sun.

It was twilight by the time he got to Carrie's gravel

driveway. He stopped, regarding the light that shone from the windows. She didn't seem to be in the living room. Maybe he could just sneak in and take Noah from his sofa-cushion pen. That is, if Noah was in it. Or he could grab the baby if Carrie wasn't right there in the kitchen or if the dogs didn't bark or if the baby didn't cry. *If, if, if, if.*

He walked quietly toward the farmhouse, careful to stay on the lawn to avoid the crunch of gravel under his sneakers. The long boards on the porch steps creaked under his weight, but by now, he could hear the blast of a commercial coming from a television. Nobody could hear him over that much noise.

He'd never seen the TV on before, and its absence had always made Carrie's place seem kind of peaceful. But now, the ad for debt consolidation that boomed through the windows and walls made him think of his grandmother, who lived with the TV on. She must be wondering where he was, and he felt bad about making her worry.

Kurt peeked in the windows and saw that Teddy—no, Noah—was lying in his cushion pen, asleep. *How could anyone sleep with all that noise?* He grabbed the porch rail and felt something damp, then saw his shirt hanging there. Carrie had washed it for him, just like she said she would. But the uneasiness in Kurt's belly grew. He knew that no matter what he did now, he was going to hurt somebody.

He turned the knob and pushed the door open, but teetered back a step as the blast of noise and the awful reek hit him full in the face. He looked around. There was Buddy, chewing on a hunk of leather something. A boot or a purse, probably. The little dog looked up, but didn't come to greet Kurt or even wag his tail. Penny lay not too far away, shredding a scrap of plaid fabric. She didn't seem interested in him, either.

But it was the piles of dog poop that made him stare, then cover his nose and mouth, breathing through his fingers so as not to vomit. *What happened here since this afternoon?*

Kurt ducked his head around to peer into the kitchen. Mavis raised her head, ears up, at the sight of him. Carl slept at her side under the kitchen table and didn't stir. But he saw no sign of Carrie. He took one more breath through his fingers and then held it against the smell. He ran back to the sleeping baby, not sure how much time he had.

Noah felt lighter than before, and Kurt felt the heat coming off his little body. There were dark hollows beneath his eyes, and when he opened them, they seemed blank. Kurt staggered, realizing how bad things were—the sick baby, the dogs, the horrible smell. He had no idea what had happened to the orange cat he'd brought earlier.

What have I done?

"What are you doing?" Kurt jumped, exhaling sharply at the sound of Carrie's voice. He hadn't heard her come in. It's the TV, he thought. *An elephant could have snuck up on me with all that noise.* He turned around and was shocked. Carrie's hair was still like a fright wig, and she was still wearing the same dirty clothes. But that wasn't the worst of it. It was her eyes that scared him. They glittered as if backlit, settling first on him, then on the baby. They darted over the rest of the room, then came back to him. And her hands moved in time to some inner music that Kurt couldn't hear. *This isn't Carrie!*

"I came to get the baby, Carrie." Kurt pulled himself up to his full height, too freaked out now by the frightening presence before him to notice the smell anymore.

"It's dinnertime," she said. And before he could react, Carrie snatched Noah from his grasp. She spun around and went into the kitchen.

Puddles of animal pee lay by the door to the backyard and to the garage, and Kurt gingerly stepped over a pile of poop, trying to stay near the baby.

"Carrie," he tried again. "I need to take the baby back."

But Carrie didn't answer. She didn't even seem to hear him. Placing the baby on one hip, she took a can of dog food from the cupboard, clicked it into the electric can opener, then pressed the lever.

Buddy and Penny came racing into the kitchen at the sound of the whir, but Carrie kicked them away. Kurt noticed that Mavis and Carl never moved from their spot beneath the table.

Kurt watched Carrie yank open a drawer, take out a spoon, slam the drawer shut, release the can from the opener, then set it on the counter. She kicked once more at the clamoring, hungry dogs, snarling a sharp "No!"

"Let me have the baby, Carrie. Please let me have Noah." He took a step closer.

"His name," she said, fixing him with her bright and terrible eyes, "is Teddy!" She rammed the spoon into the open can, scooped up a brown mushy mound, and brought it to the baby's lips. Kurt watched in horror as Noah opened his mouth as obediently as a baby bird, then took the dog food and swallowed.

Now, this was not a world Kurt understood. Unable to hold back any longer, he succumbed, vomiting on the kitchen floor.

As Penny and Buddy fell over themselves to lap up the mess at his feet, Kurt lunged at Carrie and the baby. But she moved aside more quickly than he expected, and Noah started to scream. Kurt reached out to yank the baby away from her when her free hand whipped back. Before he could raise a hand to protect himself, Carrie grabbed the electric can opener, yanked it from the wall, and crashed it down, right on the side of his head.

"You little SOB," Mark said as Kurt punched him in the side of his head.

But he hadn't hit Mark this hard, because now, Kurt could barely stand. And he could no more grab Carrie's arms or the baby than he could fly to the moon. *Is this what they mean by seeing stars?* The flashes of light dancing before him were as pretty as the sparkles he saw in the sky. But they really didn't look like stars at all.

Then Kurt fell hard, catching his left arm beneath him. To his surprise, he could hear the snap of bone over the television noise and the crying baby. He found himself on the floor and thought he saw a brown and black shape hovering over him. *Mavis?* But then she was gone. He felt himself lifted and dragged by the collar, the sudden blinding pain in his arm making those pretty lights dance once more.

It was the middle of the night, and Will couldn't sleep. But he forced himself to stay in bed in the dark, hoping to

LISTEN

bore himself enough to nod off. Terrible images of Kurt's burn-scarred arm, along with the gruesome story of Carrie Williams, kept his brain wired and alert. Turning over again, he noted that just 17 minutes had passed since the last time he had checked his clock. Praying for sleep or daylight, not really caring which, Will squeezed his eyes shut, trying to empty his mind.

Three minutes later, he looked again, then turned his pillow to find a cool spot. He started thinking about the quiet, empty house. How long had it been since anyone else had slept here? He counted off the months and stopped at seven.

If only he'd yelled at his brother, or punched him, or tackled him that day, maybe he wouldn't be alone now. He turned his pillow again.

Had anyone done that for Kurt? Tried to stop the person who burned him like that? They didn't help him when his arm got messed up, that's for sure. At least I'm helping him with his grades. At least I'm being nice to him.

Nice? Even thinking that word made him sick. It didn't require an awful taste to make him feel that way. Besides, *nice* had no taste; it was nothing. *Nice* wouldn't change the reality of those nasty red scars on Kurt's arm, and it wouldn't make them better, either.

But was it his job to make things better for Kurt? Will used to wish it was someone's job to do something to make his family better when everything seemed so hopeless. *Maybe*, he thought, *Kurt wishes that now*.

He looked at the clock once more. Why did time always move so slowly when you couldn't sleep? His thoughts returned to Kurt and to the schoolwork they'd worked on together that afternoon. When he'd begun reading Kurt's short story, scrawled in chicken scratches, Will was amazed at how quickly the kid had gotten so much down on paper. *Somebody's got a lot to say*, he'd thought when Kurt handed over three filled pages. Kurt's chicken scratches made his story hard to follow, and the subject was so odd. It was kind of like a fairy tale—an ordinary good versus evil story. It was something about a king, followed by a mean king and a witch, and some sort of hidden castle. As Will felt his breathing slow and welcomed the floaty lightness of falling asleep, he suddenly remembered the rest. It was something about some kind of quest, with a prince rescuing a baby. That's when Will's eyes flew open: *a baby!*

First, there was Kurt's list of synonyms and antonyms. *Bad mother* was on that list. It was just a strange choice of words at the time. But then . . . the fast-food place: *"Your baby's crying."* And that suitcase Kurt was lugging around . . . Suddenly, it loomed large in Will's mind. Then the folded check from Carrie Williams, the one still sitting in Will's pocket that he'd found after Kurt bolted from lunch. *"I work for a lady out there. I was just bringing her something she wanted."*

Kurt, thought Will, staring at the dark ceiling as if it could tell him something more, what have you been carrying around in that suitcase of yours?

Will lay in his bed, waiting for morning. Why did time always move so slowly in the middle of the night?

~

Carrie paced in circles in the living room, holding the sleeping Teddy in her arms. The television with the volume turned up as high as it would go still didn't drown out the accusations flying at her from all sides.

"He's hurt, Carrie." Carl stared at her endlessly from his perch on her easy chair.

"Get off my chair, Carl," she muttered, making another round through the room.

"You have to help him," the three-legged cat insisted.

"I *said* get off my chair!" Carrie hurled a sofa cushion at the cat, but missed by a foot or more.

"You hurt him. We saw you!" Penny whined.

"Help him, we need to help him." Buddy stuck close to the dachshund's side. "Carrie, why won't you help him?"

"Shut up! All of you, just shut up!" The baby awoke and began to cry again, but his thin wails didn't bother her now. Soon, the dogs stopped their arguments, leaving only the noise from the television and the baby in her arms. She turned down the volume by half.

Thump. Thump. "Carrie," came a muffled cry from down the hall.

"You shut up, too!" she yelled in the direction of the bathroom. She returned the TV volume to full blast, then resumed her pacing, careful to avoid Mavis's silent steady gaze from her place under the kitchen table. "I need to keep moving," Carrie said into Teddy's sweat-dampened hair. "Everything will be all right, as long as I just keep moving."

∼

The cool tile floor felt good beneath him when Kurt managed to shake the fog from his brain. He was in Carrie's bathroom. She must have locked him in. She probably thought he'd try to run away. Well, she'd be right about that, but he wasn't going without Noah.

Oh, god. Noah! The feeling of nausea rose up at the memory of Carrie spooning dog food into the baby's mouth. Bringing his hands up to his face, Kurt discovered that pain, too, was making him feel like losing it once more. His throbbing left arm was swollen, the purple almost obscuring his scars. He tried wiggling his fingers, but they remained still, curled slightly against his palm. Carrie had done what even Mark couldn't manage—she'd broken one of his bones.

Kurt struggled to his feet and tried the knob with his good hand. It felt jammed, and after pushing it with his shoulder and kicking it a couple of times, he knew the solid door wasn't going to budge. And by the sound of the TV, muffled even through the bathroom door, he knew nobody'd hear any noise he might make.

Kurt slowly turned around, taking in the rest of the bathroom. Toilet, shower-curtained bathtub, sink, mirror, medicine cabinet, and window. The window was small, up near the ceiling, and the thick layers of paint over the latch meant it hadn't been opened in a long time. But Kurt had a lot of experience getting in and out of windows, which gave him the confidence to try.

He climbed up on the lid of the toilet seat, but reaching up caused him such pain that he almost passed out again. He gingerly got down, then opened the medicine cabinet in search of something to stop the throbbing in his head and arm. But what he found there confused him. Instead of the usual Band-Aids, Pepto-Bismol, or aspirin, all three shelves were filled with prescription pill containers. Kurt picked one up and knew it was empty before even shaking it.

Kurt ran his finger down the line to the last bottle on the shelf. Unlike all of the others, this one was almost full. He read the date and dosage, and he knew that Carrie should have taken all these pills by now. Kurt closed the cabinet and sat down on the tiles again, already tired from the effort, and leaned his head against the edge of the bathtub.

So what did it mean? If she'd taken that last bottle of pills, would he be trapped here, injured, in her bathroom?

Only a couple of days ago, Kurt had thought she was strange but nice, and she had seemed like she actually cared about him. So did one bottle of pills make such a difference? His head ached and his arm throbbed in answer: he was hurting all over. Then he thought of his mom. Drugs had made a huge difference with her. It must be the opposite deal with Carrie: without these drugs she's not just strange, she's dangerous.

Thinking about all this exhausted Kurt more than ever in his life. He closed his eyes, but then screamed when the shower curtain moved against the back of his head. Two large green eyes appeared over the rim of the tub, and Kurt leapt up to pull back the plastic as the orange tabby deftly leapt out and onto the floor. Kurt dropped down beside it, and the cat crawled right into his lap.

They sat there together, Kurt stroking the orange fur with his good hand. "I want my grandmother," he told the cat, surprising himself at the words. His eyes grew heavy and closed. Much later, he woke himself up, calling "Mom."

Pain raced up his arm, and his head still hurt, joined now by his neck. *Bathtubs don't make very good pillows*, he thought. The noise from the TV continued, and Kurt was shocked to see daylight through the little bathroom window. He moved the cat off his lap and tried the door again: still shut tight. When the volume on the television fell, Kurt waited to see whether it was just a show ending. But the volume was truly down. He thumped the door with the side of his foot, calling, "Carrie!" The cat, startled, jumped back into the tub.

"You shut up, too!" The shriek didn't even sound like Carrie's voice.

Kurt took another breath to yell again, but the TV volume shot back up. Then he looked down at the cat. "What have I done to you?" he asked. Seeing his own ragged reflection in the mirror over the sink, he thought of Noah and Buddy, too. "What have I done to us all?"

When Will realized Kurt was five minutes late, he knew the kid wasn't coming. He picked up his backpack and headed to the office. "I'm his student mentor," he told the secretary when she told him that Kurt was indeed absent. "I need to get his work to him," he insisted when the secretary said she couldn't give out Kurt's address. But the girl volunteer caught up with him in the hallway and told him Kurt lived two houses from hers.

Will ran to the parking lot. He didn't realize until he parked in front of the small house that he had no idea what he was going to say if Kurt was home. What was he going to do? Yell "Stop, put up your hands?"

Will switched off the ignition. Should he have called Claire first? She wasn't at school again. *No*, he thought. If he was wrong about Kurt, she'd think he was an idiot—and a creepy one at that.

But if he turned out to be right, maybe she'd think he was some kind of hero. He relished the taste of baked ham the word *hero* evoked, but he could hardly bring himself to hope. The warm taste intensified as he considered what it could mean if she ended up thinking of him that way.

But he could be responsible for getting Kurt busted, too. The kid was no monster; he was sure of that. Most of the time, he just seemed very defensive. And after seeing the scars on his arm, who could blame him? Will wasn't at all sure this was what he should be doing, but he couldn't sit in his car all day and do nothing.

No. This time I'm going to do something.

He left his car and walked quickly up to the front door, but it opened before he could knock. The grandmother stood in the open doorway, looking like she was about to lose it.

"Will?" she asked. "You're Will, aren't you? Kurt's friend?" She spoke quickly and looked past him, hope in her eyes. "Is Kurt with you, Will? Is he in the car?"

"Uh, no." Will hadn't expected to be ambushed by Kurt's grandmother on the front porch, so he hurriedly collected his thoughts before going on. "He wasn't at school today, and I need to talk to him about an, um, assignment." He fought a wince at the awful taste that word left on his tongue. Why couldn't he remember to say *paper* instead?

"He wasn't at school?" Now her face was full of worry. "Then I don't know where he could be. I've been up all night, waiting for him. When I saw you drive up, I hoped he was with you."

"He hasn't been here *all night*?" Will tried to remember what time he'd seen Kurt at the restaurant. It had been around five or so when Kurt bolted from the table. "I saw him at around five o'clock yesterday. Wasn't he here after that?"

She took a pack of cigarettes and a yellow plastic lighter out of her pocket. "It was earlier, after school. He was so upset when he left. I thought he was just going off like he does sometimes—to cool off, you know." She lit the cigarette with shaky hands.

"Didn't you call anybody?" Will could hear his voice rising. He would *never* let his kid go missing overnight without calling the police. Will's eyes drifted to the cigarette, and she followed his gaze. Maybe she knew something she didn't want the police to know.

"How did Kurt get those burns on his arm?"

She straightened, and her eyes grew hard. "If you think

I had anything to do with hurting that boy, you're wrong!" She angrily threw her cigarette down and ground it out with her foot. "Kurt's mother made some sorry decisions in her life, and that monster of a boyfriend was the worst of them. I'm sure Kurt's told you those stories."

"Yeah," Will replied, hoping she'd tell him more. "The boyfriend. Is that why Kurt didn't come home?" Will didn't understand what had happened. *Did the boyfriend take the baby?*

She frowned and shook her head. "He can't do anything to Kurt anymore. Bad enough he was beating up Kurt's mom. And then he went after a *boy*. Kurt did what he had to do to protect himself from that monster." Her expression hardened with her words.

At this, Will's mouth went dry. "What did Kurt do?"

She looked unsure. "What did Kurt tell you about it?"

Will shrugged, hoping to look noncommittal. "Just some stuff." Technically, that wasn't a lie. Kurt had told him plenty in his writing.

"So he told you what happened with that miserable excuse for a man?"

Will nodded, thinking about Kurt's odd short story. What was the word he'd used? *Vanquished.* That was it. It stood out right away, first because of the strong black cherry taste and then because of the impressive choice of words. "He told me he got rid of him."

She looked off over his shoulder and sounded more like she was talking to herself. "When he stabbed him, it was self-defense. That's exactly what it was. Not only that, but he saved his mother. It was only a matter of time before

177

that man would have killed her." Her eyes filled with tears. "That Kurt does as well as he does, well, it's a miracle to me."

Stabbed him? Like, stabbed dead? Will hid his reaction. *If Kurt's capable of something like that, then . . . Maybe I should just call the police.*

"Do you have any idea where he might be? This, um, paper we're working on, it's pretty important." Will sounded as earnest as he could, considering what he'd just found out. He needed to figure out where Kurt was, now even more than before.

"He did say he was bringing a cat to the lady he's been working for, but I don't know her name." A new look of hope crossed her face. "Do you know who she is?"

He nodded. *I know way more about her than I want to, that's for sure.* "I can go check at her house if you want." *No. I should call the cops as soon as I get out of here.*

She breathed a relieved sigh. "Bless you, Will. Thank you. You don't know what it means to know Kurt has a friend like you."

Will hoped this would be easy and that Kurt would answer the door, look at him like he was crazy, and then say get lost. Or maybe he would consider Will to be some kind of hero and then tell him where the baby was. Will shook his head inwardly. What was he expecting? Some sort of freaking parade in his honor? Where he and Claire would ride in a convertible, crowns on their heads, waving to the cheering crowd? How dumb was that?

Now, thanks to Kurt's grandmother, with her guilt-inducing remark, Will had to do one more thing before turning in the kid.

Will mulled over these thoughts as he left the old lady on the porch and got in his car. But as he drove out of town, he couldn't get the image of these two newly discovered Kurts out of his mind. Was he Kurt the mother-saving hero or Kurt the knife-wielding killer?

In all the time he'd spent with Kurt, Will never would've pegged him as either one. But he'd never expected to be heading to Crazy Carrie's house, the one straight out of his childhood nightmares, trying to track down the missing kid and the stolen baby, either. So go figure.

"All right, Mavis, enough is enough." Carrie squatted down to speak to the big dog under the table, with Teddy still wrapped tightly in her arms. She knew he'd drenched her sweatshirt with urine again, but she didn't feel cold with the baby's hot body pressed against her.

She straightened, peeved at the dog's silence. "Okay then, Carl." But Carl wasn't talking to her, either. "Penny, Buddy," she called. When the little black dog showed up at her feet, she fixed him with a glare. "Talk to me. God, I couldn't get you to shut up before!" Carrie kicked at him, and he skittered away. She spied Penny in the living room, creating another mound near the front door. "You'll all get to go out, and be fed," she said, "when someone decides to talk to me." She cast a meaningful glance at Mavis.

Carrie began pacing again, grateful now for the din of the television, not because it covered up the voices of the animals but because at least she felt like she had *some* company and that *someone* was still talking to her. She so hated being alone.

Her short, quick steps brought her near the hallway, where she regarded the kitchen chair propped under the bathroom doorknob. She considered opening it, to see whether the boy was now on her side again. He'd had all night to think about it; she did a lot of her best thinking at night, and maybe he did the same. Carrie tiptoed toward the door, then rapped it. "Hello," she called.

"Yeah." The boy's voice sounded like it was right on the other side of the door. "Carrie, please let me go."

"I can't do that. Not after what you did to me." She could feel her agitation starting to return.

"I'll take the blame, Carrie." But the boy didn't sound sorry at all. "I'll bring the baby back, and no one will ever know he was here."

Carrie's eyes began to burn from the anger filling her head. "Teddy is not going anywhere." She began kicking the door. "You're just like the rest of them—Carl, Mavis, all of them. Taking, taking, that's all you do." Teddy's head lolled as Carrie's body shook with each kick. "The only people who were ever good to me, who ever *listened* to me, were my parents. Parents love you no matter *what*." She had stopped kicking, but her heart was pounding and sweat burned her eyes.

"Carrie, listen. . . . "

Carrie could hear the deceit in his tone, but it didn't bother her. Talking to the boy had given her the answer she needed. "Good-bye," she said. "You go ahead and stay here. I'll be back soon."

"Carrie!"

The boy's cries followed her down the hall and out to the kitchen. She scanned the countertop and picked up her keys. Mavis got to her feet when she heard them jingle. "You might as well forget about it," she told the dog. "You're not going anywhere."

Carrie entered the garage and tripped the door opener. Sunlight flooded the space, and she celebrated the beauty of the spring morning. It was a wonderful day, she thought, getting in the car and laying Teddy on the passenger seat. A perfect day to visit her parents.

She rolled down her window to enjoy the fresh air as she backed out into the driveway. The sound of a crash made her look back toward the house, where she saw Mavis's large form bounding across the yard. A smaller crash followed, and she put the car in Drive and turned around on the grass. Mavis was trying to catch up with the car, but Carrie knew she wouldn't make it. Stomping on the gas pedal, she saw in her rearview mirror a cloud of dust obscure the dog and the farmhouse as she left them behind.

The knocking on the bathroom door sounded as sudden and startling as a gunshot. Kurt leapt up, the orange cat hissing at his abrupt movement. "Hello," said a voice from the other side of the door.

"Yeah." Kurt felt like he could barely breathe. Tears sprouted from his eyes. "Carrie, please let me go." He was ashamed of the tears, of the almost uncontrollable fear he felt now that she was actually talking to him. He closed his eyes and thought of the petrified wood in his bedroom. Oh, he was petrified all right, scared right out of his mind. But the word also meant that something had turned to stone. And that's what he needed to be now—hard as a rock. Not like before, when being petrified meant not feeling. Now it meant more like what his dad had intended, that Kurt needed to be strong. *I'm strong as a rock*, he repeated to himself.

"I can't do that. Not after what you did to me." Carrie's voice was shrill.

Kurt concentrated on making his voice sound calm. "I'll take the blame, Carrie. I'll bring the baby back, and no one will ever know he was here." *Open the door. Open the door*. He willed her to do his bidding as his arm throbbed in time to the chant in his head.

But Carrie went nuts instead, screaming something about everybody taking things from her or something like that. He fell back a step as the door bowed inward from the force of her kicking it. Then the blows stopped, and he came closer to catch her words: "Parents love you no matter *what*."

Huh? Kurt had no idea what she was talking about. Did she mean *his* parents? After what he did to Mark, Kurt didn't think they still loved him. After all, his dad had just dumped him in this dive of a town, and his mom—well, how could he expect her to care about him anymore? She loved Mark, and Kurt had killed him.

"Carrie, listen. . . . " He kept his voice in the same even tone, trying to bring her back to the baby and the idea of letting him out.

"Good-bye," she said. Her voice sounded bright, almost normal. "You go ahead and stay here. I'll be back soon."

No. No way. "Carrie!" he yelled. "Carrie, come back!" But she didn't answer. And the screaming made his head ache. *It wasn't doing any good, anyway. All I did was scare the cat.* He reached down to try to pet the tabby.

He heard a rumble over the noise of the television. It was a familiar sound. He had trouble placing it at first, but then the revving car engine made him realize it was the garage door opening. *She really is leaving*, he thought in a panic. He had to try and stop her. A crash followed the grind of the garage door closing again, and Kurt suddenly understood what Carrie meant about parents loving you no matter what. He looked around the bathroom for the hundredth time, trying to find a way out. He stared at the small square of glass, the sparkles floating in the blue sky framed there mocking him instead of giving him comfort. It felt almost like a dare. "Come and get us," the lights seemed to say. "All you need to do is find a way out." He quickly scooped the orange cat up with his good hand, putting him back in the tub and closing the plastic shower curtain. Then he yanked off his sneaker and threw.

The yellow farmhouse sure doesn't look like something nightmares are made of, Will thought as he pulled into the driveway. As he walked up to the porch, blue fabric hanging over the rail caught his eye. It was the long-sleeved shirt Kurt always wore.

Even outside on the porch, the sound of a TV talk show blasted. *Well, if someone bad's living here, their hearing isn't so good.*

Will knocked on the door and called "Hello" a couple of times. Still getting no answer, he turned the knob and walked in.

The smell rocked him. And for a second, Will forgot he wasn't eight years old, hearing his mom tell the story of the horror his uncle had found there that terrible day. But this time, it wasn't death he smelled. *No, it's* . . . He walked in and felt something squish beneath his shoe. *Oh, shi . . .* Catching himself mid-word, Will ran outside to frantically scrape his tennis shoe on the grass. Going back inside, he was careful where he stepped.

"Hello?" Will called as two little dogs sniffed at his legs. They seemed friendly enough, and he reached down to pet them. "Didn't anybody housebreak you guys?" The shrill noise from the television was getting to him, and he turned it off.

"Is anybody home?" That's when he heard a sudden crash and a yelp—a decidedly human sound.

"I'm in the bathroom!" called a voice.

"Kurt?" Will looked around, trying to figure out where he was.

"Help me!" came the pleading reply.

Will followed the voice to the hallway, where he saw the chair propped against the door. "Hold on," he called as he moved the chair aside and pulled open the door. The first thing he saw was a streak of orange shooting past his legs. Then he stared at the strange sight before him. With the jagged maw of a broken window above him, Kurt stood with one shoe off and clutching a shower curtain rod. A shower curtain was twisted completely around him.

"Oh, my god, what happened, Kurt? What are you doing in here?" Will asked.

Kurt looked first at the rod and then down at the tangle of plastic. "Trying to escape." Then he burst into tears and collapsed.

The car rolled smoothly down the road as Carrie hummed a bit of a lullaby her mother used to sing. Teddy opened his eyes and pulled at his ear, making small mews that made Carrie smile. "You sound like a kitty. Meow." The baby then stuck a fist in his mouth and quieted down.

It really is a stellar day, she thought. Hardly a cloud in the sky, and the wildflowers are simply . . . She slammed on the brakes, reaching out to keep Teddy from flying off the seat. An azure stand of bachelor buttons by the side of the road had caught her eye. They'd be just the thing to take, since her mother always loved flowers and blue was her father's favorite color. She adjusted Teddy's wrappings, then got out to pick the blossoms, still contentedly humming that same sweet melody.

Now that he'd broken the window, Kurt knew he had to figure out a way to get through it, so high up on the wall.

The cat made a noise from the tub, and Kurt drew the shower curtain aside. Looking first at the cat, then up at the curtain rod, a thought formed as he held the plastic.

With his good hand, Kurt pulled on the metal rod, but it was firmly attached to the wall. He gave a harder tug, sending bits of plaster flying. Then, after moving the cat out of harm's way, Kurt braced his foot against the bathtub and yanked with all his strength.

Pain flared up his arm, and he thought the sudden silence meant he was starting to faint. But a split second later, the rod and the sheet of heavy plastic came down on top of him with a crash. He yelped in surprise, then heard someone's voice—one that didn't belong to Carrie.

"I'm in the bathroom!" he called, pushing aside the curtain and rod.

"Kurt?" the voice called out.

"Help me!" Kurt yelled, doubling the pain in his head.

Kurt heard the voice say "Hold on" as something scraped against the door. Finally, it swung open and the orange cat shot out; Kurt stared, dumbfounded at the sight of Will in the doorway.

"Oh, my god, what happened, Kurt? What are you doing in here?" Will asked. He looked as freaked out as Kurt felt.

"Trying to escape," Kurt replied. All the fear and worry crashed down on him, and he collapsed into helpless sobs.

~

Kurt's tears scared Will as much as the disgusting state of the house. He helped extricate Kurt from his plastic wrapping, and when he lifted it off the boy's arm, Kurt let out a scream.

"Whoa! Sorry. What . . . " his stomach gave a flip when he saw the arm, all swollen, lumpy, and darkly bruised. "Man," he said, "what happened to your arm?"

The two little dogs padded into the bathroom. Then the wiener dog stretched up to the open toilet bowl and drank greedily as the other dog paced and whined.

"It's Carrie. She's totally gone crazy." Kurt's words came out in bursts, forcing Will to listen carefully as he tried to make sense of them. "She has the baby," Kurt went on. "I tried to get him back, but she wouldn't let me take him. I knew I shouldn't have let him stay here, but I didn't know she'd go so crazy. I'm sorry—I really just didn't know! She said he'd be better off."

The boy's sobs made him even harder to understand, and it took a while for Will to figure things out. Even when he at last understood, things still didn't exactly make sense.

"Carrie Williams has Noah?"

Kurt swallowed hard and nodded his head.

"Is she here?" Will looked quickly back over his shoulder.

"No, she's gone. I heard her car driving away."

"We need to find the phone," Will said firmly. "We have to call the police."

Kurt nodded again and started to leave the bathroom. That's when Will noticed the matted hair over the boy's left ear; clearly, it was dried-up blood.

"Oh," Will said quietly, hating that his voice sounded weak. "We need to get you to the hospital—now."

But Kurt was already down the hall. When Will caught up with him, he was standing in the kitchen before the broken window. Shattered glass lay in puddles of urine, and sharp spears jutted out from the window frame.

"Carrie jumped out the window?" Will asked, perplexed. *No. She wouldn't have thrown a baby out, would she?* He looked anxiously at the tall grass below.

"Did you see a German shepherd around here?" Kurt picked a piece of fluff from the jagged glass in the window frame, then looked around the kitchen "Mavis?" he called.

"A German shepherd?" Will didn't mind dogs, as long as they were a lot smaller than he was. "Is she friendly?" He scanned the kitchen quickly, too, but saw only the wiener dog and the little black mop.

"Mavis jumped out the window. She was trying to follow Carrie." Kurt opened the door and bolted outside. "I have to find her."

Find her? Find who, Carrie or the dog?

"Kurt!" Will shouted after him. The kid had a broken arm and blood on his head, and why was he wearing only one shoe? "Um, stay," he said to the two dogs, then made sure he closed the door tightly. He got to his car just as Kurt ran onto the road. Will left a spray of gravel in his wake as the station wagon hit the road; then he pulled over next to Kurt. "Get in. Now!" he ordered.

"Why should I do anything you say?" Kurt shot back, his mouth twisted into an attempted snarl. Instead, he looked pathetic.

"You see anyone else here with a car?"

Kurt looked up and down the deserted road, but made no move to get in.

"I know you killed that guy. Your grandmother told me, Kurt. It's okay."

Kurt's face whitened even more, and Will wanted to kick himself. *Well, aren't you just the world's best negotiator, William. Why don't you tell him he's ugly and smells bad while you're at it?*

"My brother killed someone, too." It was the first time Will had ever said it out loud. And it didn't feel nearly as bad as when he'd said it in his head so many times before, much to his surprise.

"No kidding?" Kurt replied with sarcasm. "I just moved here, and even I know that." But then he got in the car, and Will swallowed his pain at the kid's snotty tone. *I really am such a baby, sometimes.*

"So what's this supposed to be? Some kind of club, for killers or their brothers?" the boy went on, snidely.

Will ignored his remarks, studying Kurt's face and his shirt, both of which were wet with perspiration. His color was terrible, and from the looks of that arm and the wound on his head, the boy was probably going into shock. Will took his cell phone from the glove box, saying, "I'm calling the police, and we're going straight to the hospital."

"I know where she went," Kurt said.

"Where?" Will hit "9" on the keypad.

"She went to go see her parents."

Will groaned inwardly. Apparently, Carrie Williams wasn't the only crazy person he was dealing with here. "The Williamses are dead," he replied, hitting the first "1" on the keypad.

"I *know* they're dead, Will." Kurt's adolescent-edgy voice was razor sharp. "She's going to the *cemetery*."

"The cemetery?" Will's finger hovered over the keypad.

"I don't know the name of it. There's lots of really old graves there." Kurt's words grew ever more urgent. "It's kind of overgrown, and there's a long gravel road leading up to it. We have to go there now! She's taken Noah with her!"

Will knew the cemetery. His mother was buried there. He hit the final "1" on the phone. "Police," he stated calmly to the operator.

The rest of the brief call seemed so surreal that Will wondered whether he was actually awake. *How long can nightmares last?* Yes, he told the police dispatcher. He knew who had Noah Lemay. He was pretty sure he knew where that person was now, and yes, as far as he knew, the child was still alive. He gave his name and contact information, then clicked off the phone.

He turned to Kurt. "Now we're going to the hospital."

"No!" The boy shouted, his eyes boring right into Will. "I have to go to the cemetery. I have to get that baby back!"

Will paused. Then, with his hand before Kurt's eyes, he asked, "How many fingers?"

"Three!" the boy responded, irritated.

"Oh, crap," Will said when the boy answered correctly, the taste of ick filling his mouth. He hit the gas, and speeding the old car faster than it had probably ever gone before, he headed toward the cemetery. He was pretty sure Kurt would be okay until they met the police at the graveyard. But another thought eclipsed even that as the station wagon raced past trees and fields. *Is this how I finally show Claire who I really can be?*

~

Carrie stripped the urine-soaked dress shirt off Teddy and left it on the hood of her car to dry. The air was already quite warm, so it wasn't as if he really *needed* clothes now. She cuddled the quiet baby and reached back into the car to retrieve the flowers. With arms full, she made her way up to the graves.

Oh, no. She had forgotten to bring water. She reprimanded herself as she removed the dead roses from their vases, putting the bachelor buttons in their place anyway. She'd just have to come back later with the water.

Carrie sat down with the baby on the grass between the headstones, knowing from the sense of well-being that flooded her heart that this was exactly where she needed to be. They were all together again, just like before.

"See, I told you I'd make it all better." Carrie directed her statement to the blue sky rather than to the headstones. "I had to save a *baby*. It was the only thing that could make up for . . . that time." She tried to push those dark thoughts back into the past, where she knew they belonged. But they insisted; those dark thoughts always insisted.

She hadn't believed it when the nurse told her that her father was dead. She didn't believe it even when the doctor pulled the sheet up over her father's face. She had no real memory of driving herself home. . . . There hadn't been anyone to call to come and get her. There hadn't been anyone to call, even to say that her father had followed her mother in death.

191

Everything after that was lost to her. She remembered the gnawing in her belly, which she hadn't connected to hunger. She remembered the cries of her dogs and cats, whom she hadn't had the strength to check on. She remembered the smell, too, but by then, it had been too late. . . .

The hospital where they sent her was bright white. The nurses were cheerful even as they forced food down her throat. After months of pills, talking to the kind man every day, and more pills, they at last let her return home. She'd returned to the empty house and the new little graves in the yard. Walter McCarty had taken care of it for her. It was a neighborly thing to do.

But those pills took away a part of her, a special part, she'd always felt. She was right to walk away from those pills, this time for good. She looked down at the baby in her arms as Teddy again pulled at his ear. It didn't matter if Mavis, Carl, or even the new ones were done talking to her, now. She didn't need their conversations anymore. She smiled at the flush-faced infant. "It won't be long before you'll be talking to me again, will it, Daddy?" Her heart was full almost to bursting at the anticipation of it all.

Carrie frowned as the sound of a car hitting the gravel road made her look up, annoyed at the intrusion.

"Carrie!" A voice wafted up the hill. She shrank down next to the headstones, clutching Teddy close. It was the boy—Kurt!

∼

In any other situation, Kurt would have relished going this fast. His dad used to have an old Triumph convertible he was always working on, and if it was running on a sunny weekend, they'd hit the back roads, taking corners so quick that Kurt's stomach leaped into his throat. Mark had been more of the monster-truck type, and it suited him. Mark acted like a monster toward Kurt's mom, and after a while, Kurt started to see him as one.

The landscape flew past as Will sped toward the cemetery.

"Did you mean to do it?" Will asked.

"Mean to do what?" The question brought Kurt back to the present.

"Kill that guy."

Kurt shrugged. "I wanted him to stop. I wasn't thinking about anything but making him stop hurting my mom."

Will glanced over at Kurt and saw the burn scars through the bruising. *What about wanting to make him stop hurting you?*

The car suddenly swerved, and Kurt grabbed the door handle, gasping from the pain in his broken arm.

"Sorry. Dog," Will said.

"Where?" asked Kurt. "Did you hit it?"

"It's back there. And *no*, I didn't hit it," Will said, sounding irritated.

Kurt turned around and saw the German shepherd loping along the shoulder of the road. "Stop!" he yelled.

Will jammed on the brakes, sending the car into a skid. Kurt smelled the rubber on the road.

"What? What is it?" Will asked frantically.

"That's Mavis. We have to get her."

They watched the big dog run to close the gap between them, and Kurt got out of the car.

"No," said Will. "She's all dirty. Kurt . . . ?"

But Kurt bent down to receive the exhausted dog. There was blood on her fur, but other than that, she looked okay. He opened the back door, and she leapt in.

Kurt got back in, too, avoiding Will's gaze as the car picked up speed. "Did your brother mean to do it?" he asked.

Will thought for a second, back to that day at the grocery store, his mind speeding through the months leading up to it. Then he made a decision and simply answered no as he turned sharply into the cemetery's gravel road.

"That's it," said Kurt. "That's Carrie's car."

Now that they were actually here, Will wondered what he was supposed to do. The cops weren't even there yet.

Kurt opened the car door, straining his ears and hoping to hear sirens in the distance.

"Carrie!" Kurt yelled as he got out and slammed the car door.

Will began to follow, but first, looking at the dog in the back seat, left the car windows open halfway. Then he took off after Kurt. The kid was already halfway up the hill, and despite all of Will's recent running, he had trouble catching up.

Out of breath, his heart pounding, Will stopped short on the rise and stood next to Kurt, startled at what he saw. The wild-haired woman cowered against the two large headstones behind her. But Will was more interested in the naked baby she was clutching to her chest. It was Noah all right, but he was a very different baby from the chubby, gurgling one he'd seen not long ago. This baby was thinner, and his face was no longer so round. The change made him seem unnervingly adult, even old.

Kurt stepped forward, his good arm extended as if in a plea. "Carrie, please. I promise I'll take care of him."

"No!" the woman shrieked, clutching the child even tighter. Noah squirmed in her grasp and then began to cry.

Putting his hand on Kurt's shoulder, Will signaled for him to stop. Then, forcing a smile to his face, Will called out, "Ms. Williams?" Carrie snapped toward his direction, and Noah's cries rose in pitch. "It's nice to see you, Ms. Williams. I'm Will Miller. My uncle was a good friend of your dad's. You must remember him: Walt, Walt McCarty." He waited until a look of recognition flitted across Carrie's features, which were beginning to look calmer.

"Walter?" she asked.

"Yep," he nodded. "He thought the world of your family. It broke his heart when your parents passed away. He wanted to help you then, and I'm here to help you now."

"Help me?"

Will nodded again, inching his way forward as he caught the wail of sirens from the road below. "That baby sure looks heavy, Ms. Williams. Why don't you let me take him for you?"

She glared in Kurt's direction. "He wants to take Teddy."

Teddy? Will's eyes wandered to the carved letters spelling out *Theodore* above her head. "Your father was a fine man. Uncle Walt always spoke so highly of him," Will said, his own voice so calm it creeped him out. He moved his foot forward another few inches. "Why don't you let me hold the little guy for a minute?"

The instant Will saw Carrie relax, he lunged. She let out a shriek and tried to claw at his face, letting go of the baby with one hand. It was a small opening, but it was enough. Will grabbed Noah, passing him like a football to Kurt, and then went to grab hold of Carrie. With Will hanging on to one arm, she slashed at him again. This time her nails raked the side of his neck, and he covered the sting with his other hand.

"Get him in the car!" he yelled to Kurt while Carrie screamed and spit. Kurt took off down the hill. And despite Will's outweighing Carrie by a good 50 pounds, she managed to slip from his grasp. Bowling Will over on her way down the hill, Carrie shot after the fleeing Kurt.

Will bounded up and followed Carrie. He could see Kurt near the car as Carrie ran to catch him. As Will watched the line of police cars finally come into the cemetery, something else moving caught his eye.

The muffled crack of safety glass didn't seem connected to the dog hurtling from his car. She hit the ground running, and Will didn't want to see what he was sure was coming next.

Kurt seemed to sense what was about to happen, too. He stopped his mad dash and stood there, staring wide-eyed at the woman as the big dog ran to follow her.

The first police car, lights flashing and siren wailing, pulled into the road too fast, skidding on the loose gravel.

The car hit the dog with such force that her body flew in the air, spinning in a horrible arc across the brilliant spring sky.

Her arms empty, Carrie spun into a frenzy. This person was not who he represented himself to be. Walter McCarty was a good man. He would never have played a trick like this on her. And that boy now had Teddy, and she had to get him back. She *had* to get him and take him back home.

The stranger held onto her arm, but she struck out at him in a rage. He was easy to shake off, and she practically flew down the hill after the boy and Teddy. Kurt was right in front of her now, but she was startled as something hurled itself through the air. The big form of Mavis materialized at the edge of her vision, and Carrie was perplexed; Mavis was at home. Then a twinge of doubt grew as the memory of the sound of crashing glass flitted through her mind.

Now wailing filled her ears, and lights, bright with blue and red, twirled before her eyes. The boy suddenly stopped, making Carrie pause, too, confused and troubled by his expression. She turned to follow his gaze just in time to see Mavis hit square in the side by the police car. The dog's body flipped, then dropped to the ground.

"Mavis!" Carrie screamed. She ran back and knelt on the sharp stones beside her friend. Carrie could hear the sound of the radios and men yelling, but the words made no sense to her.

Mavis moved her paws jerkily, as if she were somehow still running, perhaps chasing rabbits in her dreams.

She opened her eyes slightly, but then all movement stopped. The big dog was silent, dead.

"Mavis!" Carrie raised her head to the sky and howled her anguish to the heavens.

Kurt ran with all his strength, ignoring the pain of his bare foot and broken arm as he carried the baby toward the safety of Will's car. Behind him, he heard Carrie's footsteps pounding, and he heard the cop car sirens, too. Both sounds kept him moving; he knew the police were coming for him.

But there was something else, too—a prickly feeling inside him, some fragment of fear that something terrible was coming that formed at the base of his spine and worked its way up his back. He'd always somehow felt that uneasiness when Mark was about to come after him, and now it stopped him in his tracks. He turned around.

Seeing Kurt stop made Carrie halt in her tracks, and she turned around, too. Then Kurt saw it coming. There was Mavis, running, her body stretched out in full stride. Suddenly, she was airborne as the cop car hit her broadside.

"No!" Kurt screamed, his whole world seeming to die with the great dog as she landed with a thud.

Will stopped as soon as the cop told him to halt, putting his hands behind his head as the officer patted him down. "Officer, that kid, Kurt," he gasped, "he's hurt. He needs to go to the hospital. He's got a broken arm. . . . "

"We'll take care of it," the cop said. Then, looking at Will's driver's license, he added, "Will, I need you to wait here quietly."

Will watched as Kurt was swarmed by the officers. Kurt cried out when they took Noah from him, and Will wondered, *How could they miss that messed-up arm?*

As the police fanned out through the cemetery, Will choked back an unexpected laugh, thinking, *There's only one crazy lady around here, and I'd be happy to point her out to you.*

He stood on his toes to get a better look at how Kurt was doing, but the ring of blue uniforms obscured his view.

"He's just a kid," he tried again, addressing the cop who stood nearby.

"Let's go," was all the officer replied.

The sea of blue parted as they came down the hill, and now Will could see Kurt. He was sitting on the side of the cemetery road, sobbing. Will heard more sirens in the distance and hoped that one was an ambulance.

An officer knelt next to Kurt, and Will heard her gentle tone.

"Please, can I talk to him?" Will asked. He couldn't bear to look at the dog's body as they passed.

"What's the nature of your relationship?" the officer asked.

The nature of our relationship? The question sounded odd and even a bit lewd to him. As he thought about how to reply, Will turned to see Carrie sitting in the back of a patrol car, her eyes blank and staring right at him. He doubted that she even knew he was there.

Turning his attention back to Kurt, Will quietly said, "I'm his friend."

He'd never tasted a sadder word.

The gray veil was back. In a way, she wasn't really surprised. It had been there for as long as she could remember, hovering on the edges, waiting. Her mother had always kissed it away. And all it had taken was one warm, wonderful smile from her father to let the sunlight back into her soul. Mavis, too, had known what to say when Carrie felt out of sorts. But then Mavis had stopped talking to her, and now she was gone.

The veil didn't mean her any harm. Carrie knew this. It only wanted to take care of her, to protect her from the pain and let her know it was always there to shelter her from whatever thoughts she didn't want or need to let in. So she was never really alone, as long as she had that veil. It's where her parents lived; if she listened very carefully, she'd hear them calling her name. Carrie sat now, counting her heartbeats, counting her every breath, listening for their voices as she floated along, wrapped safely in her gray veil of stars.

"She took him. She told me she'd take better care of him than his mother did," Kurt told the cop beside him.

Then he cried out, "Ohh, no, Mavis!" Kurt couldn't

stop crying, couldn't stop the trembling that shook him so hard, it felt like the earth was quaking. And he felt colder than he'd ever been.

The police officer bent and put a hand on his shoulder. "We've got an ambulance coming for you. It'll be here very soon. Want to tell me what happened to that arm? Your head doesn't look so good, either."

"She locked me up in the bathroom after she hit me with something heavy. I couldn't do anything back, not after what happened to Mark. Oh, god, Mavis is dead, isn't she?" A new round of sobs shook his frame, and pain shot up his arm, right to the center of his brain.

"You're going to be okay." The officer's voice sounded so much like his grandmother's that Kurt looked up, almost expecting to see her face.

"The baby's all right, though, isn't he?" Kurt asked, hoping with everything in him that it was true. The officer's eyes were the same color as his grandmother's, too. Kurt searched their blue depths, desperate to hide there.

"Yeah, everything's going to be all right now." She nodded, keeping her steady hand on his shoulder.

But it isn't all right, he thought. It'll never be all right again.

Will knew he'd better go directly to the police station like they told him, but there was one thing he needed to do first.

The ambulances had already left with Noah and Kurt,

and the squad car holding Carrie Williams was gone, too. Two police cars still remained, their radios bursting with noise, their disjointed words creating a muddled mess of tastes that Will wished he could block out.

He stopped his car near Mavis's body, which still lay on the dusty ground.

"Is it all right if I take her?" he asked an officer. "The dog, I mean," Will repeated. "Is it okay if I take her away and bring her home?"

The cop weighed it for a couple of seconds. "Sure, but don't touch anything else, okay? It's a crime scene."

"Thanks. I won't." Will opened the tailgate of the wagon, then lifted the dog. She was heavy and still warm as he carefully placed her in the car. He cleaned out as much glass from the upholstery and carpet as he could. It wasn't as bad as he expected.

Will thought briefly about calling his insurance agent, and it made the corners of his lips twitch even as he felt the tears threaten to spill over. *Yes, that's right. A dog jumped through my car window. No, not out of it. Through it.* Now, that's something you just don't get to say everyday.

Will walked around the car to get in, stopping to look in the direction of his mother's grave. *I should go over there*, he thought. But instead, Will got in the car and headed to the Williams place to finish the job his uncle had started so many years ago.

He expected a big police scene at the yellow farm-house, and sure enough, two cop cars sat in the driveway, their lights flashing, as he pulled in. *Don't touch anything, okay?* Will didn't want to get in trouble, but he also couldn't leave those animals in all that filth. And by the way the dachshund went for the water in the toilet bowl, they hadn't had anything to drink for quite a while.

Will waded through the grass to the kitchen door and went in. The trooper inside was startled and suspicious at first, but then let Will in to tend to the animals.

The two little dogs mobbed him when he walked in, and Will went immediately to the kitchen sink to get them water in one of the bowls stacked there. An orange cat slunk in from somewhere else in the house. *The orange blur.* "You can't stay in here," he said to all of them, breathing through his mouth to avoid inhaling the stench.

Will opened the other door in the kitchen, guessing correctly that it went to the garage. He turned on the light and set the water bowl on the concrete floor, thinking, *There has to be something here you can eat* as he returned to the kitchen. Opening all the cupboards until he found a row of dog food cans, Will stopped short at the sight of the electric can opener. It was tipped on its side, its plug hanging down to the floor, with dried blood smeared all over it and the counter. His stomach flipped at the sight, and *crime scene* popped into his head.

He put the can back and searched for a bag of dry food. Finding it, he grabbed another two bowls and headed back to the door to the garage, nearly tripping over the gray lump that was sitting there, glaring at him from the doorway. When it got to its feet upon seeing the food bag, Will realized the cat was missing a leg. *How long do nightmares last?* The gray cat followed him into the garage and watched Will heap the bowls, the excess spilling onto the floor, the little dogs wolfing it down. The cat hobbled over, sniffed the kibble once, and then turned to glare at him once more. The orange cat appeared at his side. "Sorry," Will said. "It's dog food or nothing." Will scanned the garage and was relieved at the sight of a large shovel. He grabbed it and then left the garage, closing the door against the chewing and gulping of the starving animals.

It was a chore to haul the big dog up to the rise, but as Will wiped the dirt from his palms, he knew it was worth the trouble. He marveled at the number of graves he found there, wondering which ones his uncle had dug. The new mound of dirt that now covered Mavis was next to another fairly fresh one. Will wished he had something to mark the site. He had no idea whether Carrie would ever come back to do it herself.

Will walked back to his car with his shoes, shirt, and pants a mess. Should he stop by his house to change before going to the station? No, he thought, driving away from the farmhouse. *Who was he trying to impress, anyway?*

PART 3

Agnes Brown pulled another seedling from the plastic tray and put the young marigold into the hole she had just dug. It was a warm spring, and she needed to start pulling weeds already. It made her tired just thinking about it, and she frowned at the green shoots invading her garden.

Sitting back on her heels, she rubbed her brow with the back of her gloved hand and studied her grandson. Kurt was at the patio table a few yards away, his schoolwork in front of him. Agnes watched him write something, then scowl, turn the pencil around and erase furiously. Then he stuck the pointy end of the pencil into the cast that reached from his fingers all the way up and over his elbow.

"Get that pencil out of there, Kurt!" she warned. "You're going to get an infection if you keep doing that."

"It itches," he complained. But he withdrew the pencil, anyway.

Agnes went back to her seedlings. *It was awfully nice of Will to bring Kurt's schoolwork to the house.* Will had come by a few times after that, too.

Seeing Kurt lying there, injured like that, in the hospital had nearly broken her heart. Even through the fog of painkillers, he continued to cry. He cried for his dad, and he cried for his mom. He even cried for Mark, and he cried for someone named Mavis, too. She'd thought that was just the drugs talking, but she'd found out a lot more about her grandson since then.

When the doctor spoke to her, he had explained about the specific kind of stress that came from what had happened with Mark. It was hard to learn what that traumatic stress had done to her grandson. Agnes had heard of things like that, but she was still confused. Wasn't it from being in a war? Those were the people who got that kind of traumatic stress, not kids. And surely not Kurt.

But the doctor explained that all those years with Mark had affected Kurt the same as soldiers who'd been in a war. All those years of yelling, hitting, and, finally, the burning had taken their toll. It had traumatized him as if he'd been in battle.

A battle? Agnes supposed that's exactly what Kurt had gone through, and he was still just a boy. They'd never discussed that terrible day—the day he'd killed Mark to save his mom—the whole time he'd been staying with her. She'd assumed he probably just wanted to put it behind him and not think about it again, but maybe that wasn't so smart. Well, now she understood better, and she'd do whatever was best for her grandson, whatever it took to help him heal.

At least the baby was all right, thank god. And that woman, that poor crazy woman, she was still in the hospital. Agnes sighed. What a mess it all was.

Kurt hadn't been charged with a crime—at least not

yet, anyway. They were still waiting for word about that. He was in such a terrible state when they found him that they'd assumed he was just another one of Carrie's victims. But Kurt had set that story straight right away. He explained that he knew Carrie had taken the baby but he didn't tell anyone. And he told the police about the other things he'd done wrong, such as stealing a dog and that big orange cat, the one that had messed on her carpet. But the doctor had said those things were part of Kurt's condition—post-traumatic stress disorder, PTSD, he called it. Agnes shook her head; it was all very hard to understand.

She glanced at her watch. *Where did the afternoon go?* They had a therapy session in half an hour; they'd be going twice a week for a while. They had to get groceries, too, because Kurt's mom, Sandra, was coming tomorrow. Agnes was glad that Kurt had agreed to go along to meet his mother at the station. And in three days, her son John, Kurt's dad, would arrive. It would be a full house, but she knew they'd manage. *It will be good for Kurt to have his parents with him after everything he's been through,* she reflected.

"Kurt," she called, rising from the ground with a groan, "we need to get going."

Her grandson got up and was at her side. "I'll carry that stuff for you, Grandma." Her heart ached with tenderness as he attempted to gather the yard tools in one hand, accidentally snagging a white dandelion puff along the way. His helpful expression morphed into a mischievous glint. Taking a deep breath, he blew the tiny white parachutes into the breeze. "Make a wish, Grandma," he said.

She reached over and pulled him into a hug.

Will's Blog: So here I am, talking to myself again. But what I have to say is something I can't really tell anyone else. The cat does a pretty good job of listening, but I think he gets tired of it after a while. He's pretty cool, though. I'm keeping him through the summer, until I have to leave for college. Then my friend and his grandmother agreed they'd take him. So that's cool, too. At least then I'll know he's got a good home.

I'm thinking more and more about going away. There's not a lot left for me here. Graduation, sure, but there won't be anyone in the audience for me. I'm trying to see a good side in this, that at least there won't be any good-byes. The good-byes are all over now.

That includes Claire, I guess. She told me her family was pretty weirded out about me becoming friends with that kid Kurt. I can understand that, so fair enough. She still smiles and says hi to me at school, but there definitely was a good-bye there, too. Would it have been different if I had let her know the real me? I don't know, maybe. But the time I spent with her felt so good because it was a break from the real me. I guess that's not really a good definition of a friendship, is it? She has no idea who I am. And you know what? I really didn't know her at all, either, other than that she's nice. And that she's definitely hot and has a family that's safe and so normal; at least, they seem that way. But like I said, that good-bye is fair enough, and no hard feelings.

So lately, I've been talking to Kurt a lot, and that hasn't been hard at all. I guess it's another one of those "you had to be there" sort of things. Kurt's been to hell and back again, and as much as I hate to admit it sometimes, so have I. There's just a lot less explaining with someone who's been through horror shows like we have. And I don't have to worry about the guy feeling sorry for me, that's for sure. So is this a good definition of a friendship? I'm thinking yeah, I'm pretty sure it is.

Otherwise, it's pretty much just me and the cat now. He's good company, but I think he'd be good company for anybody. He likes to hang out all the time, and when he looks at me with that green-eyed stare, it's almost like he's talking to me. But most of the time, he's just saying it's time to eat.

The best thing about this cat, though, isn't just that he seems to like me—and did I mention he only has three legs? Anyway, the best part of this cat is his name—Carl. That's my brother's name. So even though a part of me still hates him, I get to hang out with the best part of my brother: the part that listens and is calm, that doesn't tease or threaten, or worse. It reminds me of when I was little and the good part of Carl was still there, the way this Carl is here now. And that makes it easier to remember something okay about my brother. So maybe I'm ready to start looking at the stack of letters and maybe read one or two. Carl's been sending at least one a week since they first arrested him.

I never thought of this before, but it's kind of funny now that I realize it: with all those letters he's sent that I've never read, it's almost like he's been talking to himself all this time, too. It's like there's this one really small part of us that's, I don't know, the same.

So yeah, it has been a little easier to think about him, especially the word *brother*. I'm not going to say what that taste is, but to me, it's always been the best taste in the world.

I'm going out for a run now. Maybe I'll open some of those letters when I get back. Anyway, I'm out of here. So, later.

Better yet, make that *good-bye*.

Kurt sat quietly in the passenger seat of his grandmother's Toyota. The bus station was still another 20 minutes away, but the butterflies that had been deviling his stomach all morning were now beating up a storm.

What would he say to her? *I hate you? I missed you? I'm sorry?* His therapist assured him that all those feelings could be true and that it was okay to feel different things at the same time.

His dad would be here in a few days, too. He didn't want to be mad at his dad anymore, not after what he'd said on the phone: he told Kurt he was coming just as soon as he could square it at work and just as fast as his car would go.

Would it feel weird to have both his parents in the same house again, for even a little while? He wasn't sure, so he worried about that, too.

Kurt had already decided not to go back with his dad.

Would his dad be angry when he told him he was going to stay with his grandmother? She'd seemed pretty happy about it when he told her, and he really *did* want to stay, at least for a while. He couldn't think ahead about what he wanted to do after that—he wasn't ready to go there yet. And he didn't want to think about Will leaving at the end of the summer, either. But at least he still had a few months yet to figure that one out.

Meanwhile, the butterflies continued their dance and his arm inside the cast itched more than ever. He used to think his burn scars were itchy. But he'd never really understood the meaning of the word *itch* until now. Kurt longed for something—a coat hanger, a wire, anything—to jam inside his cast just to scratch away that itch.

As his grandmother took the exit ramp off the highway, Kurt could see the low brick building of the bus station. "Do you think she's here yet?"

"Could be," she said as she pulled into the parking lot. "They said they're running on time, but you never know."

Kurt unbuckled his seat belt and got out of the car, slamming the door. His grandmother stood next to the driver's side, shading her eyes against the noonday sun. "That might be her, over there," she said.

Kurt looked through the haze of heat rising from the asphalt and saw a figure, bags in hand, standing near the entrance. The shimmering air made her seem to float above the pavement.

"Sandra! Over here!" his grandmother called, waving frantically.

His mother drew closer, and Kurt looked up to the sky.

He gazed at all the sparkles he saw there, knowing they weren't really stars. But he wished on them anyway.

Acknowledgments

There's no way I could have pulled this book off all by myself. A few words written here are not nearly enough to show my appreciation for everyone who has been my support along the way, but I guess they'll have to live with it.

My deepest gratitude goes to Judy O'Malley, aka the nit-picking queen, who saw this manuscript in a much rawer form and still believed I could actually make something of it.

Mega thanks also go to Edward Necarsulmer IV, aka the coolest agent ever, who for some strange and wonderful reason thought I really did have a novel in me.

And I will always be grateful to my fabulous publisher, Evelyn Fazio, for sticking with me and encouraging me to go that terrifically difficult but certainly needed extra mile. You rock.

On the home front, a shout-out to my trusted first reader and number one son, Jeremy. Thank you for your excellent two cents. And to my husband, Derek, don't think I didn't notice your selfless sacrifice of good nutrition in eating frozen pizza for dinner several nights a week. Thank you forever for your gift of time.

I did have one constant companion who saw me through the creation of *Listen*. At nine pounds of heart-breaking cuteness, wiener dog extraordinaire Dutch provided the heart and voice of Penny. He also chewed up my pens and insisted on sleeping on my lap while I tried to type. Now that I think about it, maybe I won't thank him so much after all.

To everyone else—and you know who you are—I love you.